Langston Hughes

● *Laughing*

TO KEEP FROM

Crying

NEW YORK

HENRY HOLT AND COMPANY

B.C.
814
H

I wish to thank the editors of the following magazines for permission to reprint a number of the stories included in this book which first appeared in their pages: *The African, American Spectator, The Anvil, The Crisis, Esquire, Flight, Negro Story, New Theatre, Scribner's Fiction Parade, Stag,* and *Story Magazine.* The story "Why, You Reckon?" appeared originally in *The New Yorker.*

TO DOROTHY

● *Contents*

Contents

When you see me laughing
I'm laughing to keep from crying.

TRADITIONAL BLUES

Who's Passing
for Who?

● *ONE* of the great difficulties about being a member of a minority race is that so many kindhearted, well-meaning bores gather around to help. Usually, to tell the truth, they have nothing to help with, except their company—which is often appallingly dull.

Some members of the Negro race seem very well able to put up with it, though, in these uplifting years. Such was Caleb Johnson, colored social worker, who was always dragging around with him some nondescript white person or two, inviting them to dinner, showing them Harlem, ending up at the Savoy—much to the displeasure of whatever friends of his might be out that evening for fun, not sociology.

Friends are friends and, unfortunately, overearnest uplifters are uplifters—no matter what color they may be. If it were the white race that was ground down instead of Negroes, Caleb Johnson would be one of the first to offer Nordics the sympathy of his utterly inane society, under the impression that somehow he would be doing them a great deal of good.

You see, Caleb, and his white friends, too, were all bores. Or so we, who lived in Harlem's literary bohemia during the "Negro Renaissance" thought. We literary ones considered ourselves too broad-minded to be bothered with questions of color. We liked people of any race who smoked incessantly, drank liberally, wore complexion and morality as loose garments, and made fun of anyone who didn't do likewise. We snubbed and high-hatted any Negro or white luckless enough not to understand Gertrude Stein, Ulysses, Man Ray, the theremin, Jean Toomer, or George Antheil. By the end of the 1920's Caleb was just catching up to Dos Passos. He thought H. G. Wells good.

We met Caleb one night in Small's. He had three assorted white folks in tow. We would have passed him by with but a nod had he not hailed us enthusiastically, risen, and introduced us with great acclaim to his friends who turned out to be schoolteachers from Iowa, a woman and two men. They appeared amazed and delighted to meet all at once two Negro writers and a black painter in the flesh. They invited us to have a drink with them. Money being scarce with us, we deigned to sit down at their table.

The white lady said, "I've never met a Negro writer before."

The two men added, "Neither have we."

"Why, we know any number of *white* writers," we three dark bohemians declared with bored nonchalance.

"But Negro writers are much more rare," said the lady.

"There are plenty in Harlem," we said.

"But not in Iowa," said one of the men, shaking his mop of red hair.

"There are no good *white* writers in Iowa either, are there?" we asked superciliously.

"Oh, yes, Ruth Suckow came from there."

Whereupon we proceeded to light in upon Ruth Suckow as old hat and to annihilate her in favor of Kay Boyle. The way we flung names around seemed to impress both Caleb and his white guests. This, of course, delighted us, though we were too young and too proud to admit it.

The drinks came and everything was going well, all of us drinking, and we three showing off in a high-brow manner, when suddenly at the table just behind us a man got up and knocked down a woman. He was a brownskin man. The woman was blonde. As she rose he knocked her down again. Then the red-haired man from Iowa got up and knocked the colored man down.

He said, "Keep your hands off that white woman."

The man got up and said, "She's not a white woman. She's my wife."

One of the waiters added, "She's not white, sir, she's colored."

Whereupon the man from Iowa looked puzzled, dropped his fists, and said, "I'm sorry."

The colored man said, "What are you doing up here in Harlem anyway, interfering with my family affairs?"

The white man said, "I thought she was a white woman."

The woman who had been on the floor rose and said, "Well, I'm not a white woman, I'm colored, and you leave my husband alone."

Then they both lit in on the gentleman from Iowa. It took all of us and several waiters, too, to separate them. When it was over the manager requested us to kindly pay our bill and get out. He said we were disturbing the peace. So we all left. We went to a fish restaurant down the street. Caleb was terribly apologetic to his white friends. We artists were both mad and amused.

"Why did you say you were sorry," said the colored painter to the visitor from Iowa, "after you'd hit that man —and then found out it wasn't a white woman you were defending, but merely a light colored woman who looked white?"

"Well," answered the red-haired Iowan, "I didn't mean to be butting in if they were all the same race."

"Don't you think a woman needs defending from a brute, no matter what race she may be?" asked the painter.

"Yes, but I think it's up to you to defend your own women."

"Oh, so you'd divide up a brawl according to races, no matter who was right?"

"Well, I wouldn't say that."

"You mean you wouldn't defend a colored woman whose

husband was knocking her down?" asked the poet.

Before the visitor had time to answer, the painter said, "No! You just got mad because you thought a black man was hitting a *white* woman."

"But she *looked* like a white woman," countered the man.

"Maybe she was just passing for colored," I said.

"Like some Negroes pass for white," Caleb interposed.

"Anyhow, I don't like it," said the colored painter, "the way you stopped defending her when you found out she wasn't white."

"No, we don't like it," we all agreed except Caleb.

Caleb said in extenuation, "But Mr. Stubblefield is new to Harlem."

The red-haired white man said, "Yes, it's my first time here."

"Maybe Mr. Stubblefield ought to stay out of Harlem," we observed.

"I agree," Mr. Stubblefield said. "Good night."

He got up then and there and left the café. He stalked as he walked. His red head disappeared into the night.

"Oh, that's too bad," said the white couple who remained. "Stubby's temper just got the best of him. But explain to us, are many colored folks really as fair as that woman?"

"Sure, lots of them have more white blood than colored, and pass for white."

"Do they?" said the lady and gentleman from Iowa.

"You never read Nella Larsen?" we asked.

"She writes novels," Caleb explained. "She's part white herself."

"Read her," we advised. "Also read the *Autobiography of an Ex-colored Man*." Not that we had read it ourselves —because we paid but little attention to the older colored writers—but we knew it was about passing for white.

We all ordered fish and settled down comfortably to shocking our white friends with tales about how many Negroes there were passing for white all over America. We were determined to *épater le bourgeois* real good via this white couple we had cornered, when the woman leaned over the table in the midst of our dissertations and said, "Listen, gentlemen, you needn't spread the word, but me and my husband aren't white either. We've just been *passing* for white for the last fifteen years."

"What?"

"We're colored, too, just like you," said the husband. "But it's better passing for white because we make more money."

Well, that took the wind out of us. It took the wind out of Caleb, too. He thought all the time he was showing some fine white folks Harlem—and they were as colored as he was!

Caleb almost never cursed. But this time he said, "I'll be damned!"

Then everybody laughed. And laughed! We almost had hysterics. All at once we dropped our professionally self-conscious "Negro" manners, became natural, ate fish, and talked and kidded freely like colored folks do when there are no white folks around. We really had fun then, joking about that red-haired guy who mistook a fair colored woman for white. After the fish we went to two or three more night spots and drank until five o'clock in the morning.

Finally we put the light-colored people in a taxi heading downtown. They turned to shout a last good-by. The cab was just about to move off, when the woman called to the driver to stop.

She leaned out the window and said with a grin, "Listen, boys! I hate to confuse you again. But, to tell the truth, my husband and I aren't really colored at all. We're white. We just thought we'd kid you by passing for colored a little while—just as you said Negroes sometimes pass for white."

She laughed as they sped off toward Central Park, waving, "Good-by!"

We didn't say a thing. We just stood there on the corner in Harlem dumbfounded—not knowing now *which* way we'd been fooled. Were they really white—passing for colored? Or colored—passing for white?

Whatever race they were, they had had too much fun at our expense—even if they did pay for the drinks.

Something in Common

HONG KONG. A hot day. A teeming street. A mélange of races. A pub, over the door the Union Jack.

The two men were not together. They

came in from the street, complete strangers, through different doors, but they both reached the bar at about the same time. The big British bartender looked at each of them with a wary, scornful eye. He knew that, more than likely, neither had the price of more than a couple of drinks. They were distinctly down at the heel, had been drinking elsewhere, and were not customers of the bar. He served them with a deliberation that was not even condescending —it was menacing.

"A beer," said the old Negro, rattling a handful of Chinese and English coins at the end of a frayed cuff.

"A scotch," said the old white man, reaching for a pretzel with thin fingers.

"That's the tariff," said the bartender, pointing to a sign.

"Too high for this lousy Hong Kong beer," said the old Negro.

The barman did not deign to answer.

"But, reckon it's as good as some we got back home," the elderly colored man went on as he counted out the money.

"I'll bet you wouldn't mind bein' back there, George," spoke up the old white man from the other end of the bar, "in the good old U.S.A."

"Don't *George* me," said the Negro, " 'cause I don't know you from Adam."

"Well, don't get sore," said the old white man, coming nearer, sliding his glass along the bar. "I'm from down home, too."

"Well, I ain't from no *down home*," answered the Negro wiping beer foam from his mouth. "I'm from the North."

"Where?"

"North of Mississippi," said the black man. "I mean Missouri."

"I'm from Kentucky," vouched the old white fellow swallowing his whisky. "Gimme another one," to the bartender.

"Half a dollar," said the bartender.

"Mex, you mean?"

"Yeah, mex," growled the bartender picking up the glass.

"All right, I'll pay you," said the white man testily. "Gimme another one."

"They're tough in this here bar," said the old Negro sarcastically. "Looks like they don't know a Kentucky colonel when they see one."

"No manners in these damned foreign joints," said the white man seriously. "How long you been in Hong Kong?"

"Too long," said the old Negro.

"Where'd you come from here?"

"Manila," said the Negro.

"What'd you do there?"

"Now what else do you want to know?" asked the Negro.

"I'm askin' you a civil question," said the old white man.

"Don't ask so many then," said the Negro, "and don't start out by callin' me *George*. My name ain't George."

"What is your name, might I ask?" taking another pretzel.

"Samuel Johnson. And your'n?"

"Colonel McBride."

"Of Kentucky?" grinned the Negro impudently **tooth**less.

"Yes, sir, of Kentucky," said the white man seriously.

"Howdy, Colonel," said the Negro. "Have a pretzel."

"Have a drink, boy," said the white man, beckoning the bartender.

"Don't call me *boy*," said the Negro. "I'm as old as you, if not older."

"Don't care," said the white man, "have a drink."

"Gin," said the Negro.

"Make it two," said the white man. "Gin's somethin' we both got in common."

"I love gin," said the Negro.

"Me, too," said the white man.

"Gin's a sweet drink," mused the Negro, "especially when you're around women."

"Gimme one white woman," said the old white man, "and you can take all these Chinee gals over here."

"Gimme one yellow gal," said the old Negro, "and you can take all your white women anywhere."

"Hong Kong's full of yellow gals," said the white man.

"I mean *high-yellow* gals," said the Negro, "like we have in Missouri."

"Or in Kentucky," said the white man, "where half of 'em has white pappys."

"Here! Don't talk 'bout my women," said the old Negro. "I don't allow no white man to talk 'bout my women."

"Who's talkin' about your women? Have a drink, George."

"I told you, don't *George* me. My name is Samuel Johnson. White man, you ain't in Kentucky now. You in the Far East."

"I know it. If I was in Kentucky, I wouldn't be standin' at this bar with you. Have a drink."

"Gin."

"Make it two."

"Who's payin'?" said the bartender.

"Not me," said the Negro. "Not *me*."

"Don't worry," said the old white man grandly.

"Well, I am worryin'," growled the bartender. "Cough up."

"Here," said the white man, pulling out a few shillings. "Here, even if it is my last penny, here!"

The bartender took it without a word. He picked up the glasses and wiped the bar.

"I can't seem to get ahead in this damn town," said the old white man, "and I been here since Coolidge."

"Neither do I," said the Negro, "and I come before the War."

"Where is your home, George?" asked the white man.

"You must think it's Georgia," said the Negro. "Truth is I ain't got no home—no more home than a dog."

"Neither have I," said the white man, "but sometimes I wish I was back in the States."

"Well, I don't," said the Negro. "A black man ain't got a break in the States."

"What?" said the old white man, drawing up proudly.

"States is no good," said the Negro. "No damned good."

"Shut up," yelled the old white man waving a pretzel.

"What do you mean, shut up?" said the Negro.

"I won't listen to nobody runnin' down the United States," said the white man. "You better stop insultin' America, you big black ingrate."

"You better stop insultin' me, you poor-white trash," bristled the aged Negro. Both of them reeled indignantly.

"Why, you black bastard!" quavered the old white man.

"You white cracker!" trembled the elderly Negro.

These final insults caused the two old men to square off like roosters, rocking a little from age and gin, but glaring fiercely at one another, their gnarled fists doubled up, arms at boxing angles.

"Here! Here!" barked the bartender. "Hey! Stop it now!"

"I'll bat you one," said the white man to the Negro.

"I'll fix you so you can't leave, neither can you stay," said the Negro to the white.

"Yuh will, will yuh?" sneered the bartender to both of them. "I'll see about batting—and fixing, too."

He came around the end of the bar in three long strides. He grabbed the two old men unceremoniously by the scruff of their necks, cracked their heads together twice, and threw them both calmly into the street. Then he wiped his hands.

The white and yellow world of Hong Kong moved by, rickshaw runners pushed and panted, motor horns blared, pedestrians crowded the narrow sidewalks. The two old men picked themselves up from the dust and dangers of a careless traffic. They looked at one another, dazed for a moment and considerably shaken.

"Well, I'll be damned!" sputtered the old white man. "Are we gonna stand for this—from a Limey bartender?"

"Hell, no," said the old Negro. "Let's go back in there and clean up that joint."

"He's got no rights to put his Cockney hands on Americans," said the old white man.

"Sure ain't," agreed the old Negro.

Arm in arm, they staggered back into the bar, united to protect their honor against the British.

• *African Morning*

● MAURAI took off his calico breech-cloth of faded blue flowers. He took two buckets of water and a big bar of soap into the back yard and threw water all over himself until he was clean. Then he wiped his small golden body on an English towel and went back into the house. His mother had told him always to wear English clothes whenever he went out with his father, or was sent on an errand into the offices of the Export Company or onto one of the big steamships that came up the Niger to their little town. So Maurai put on his best white shirt and a pair of little white sailor trousers that his mother had bought him before she died.

She hadn't been dead very long. She was black, pure African, but Maurai was a half-breed, and his father was white. His father worked in the bank. In fact, his father was the president of the bank, the only bank for hundreds of miles on that part of the coast, up the hot Niger delta in a town where there were very few white people. And no other half-breeds.

That was what made it so hard for Maurai. He was the only half-native, half-English child in the village. His black mother's people didn't want him now that she was dead; and his father had no relatives in Africa. They were all in England, far away, and they were white. Sometimes when Maurai went outside of the stockade, the true African children pelted him with stones for being a half-breed and living inside the enclosure with the English. When his mother was alive, she would fight back for Maurai and protect him, but now he had to fight for himself.

In the pale fresh morning, the child crossed the large, square, foreign enclosure of the English section toward that corner where the bank stood, one entrance within the stockade and another on the busy native street. The boy thought curiously how the whites had built a fence around themselves to keep the natives out—as if black people were animals. Only servants and women could come in, as a rule.

And already his father had brought another young black woman to live in their house. She was only a child, very young and shy, and not wise like his mother had been.

There were already quite a few people in the bank this morning transacting business, for today was Steamer Day, and Maurai had come to take a letter to the captain for his father. In his father's office there were three or four assistants surrounding the president's desk, and as Maurai opened the door he heard the clink of gold. They were counting money there on the desk, a great pile of golden coins, and when they heard the door close, they turned quickly to see who had entered.

"Wait outside, Maurai," said his father sharply, his hands on the gold, so the little boy went out into the busy main room of the bank again. Evidently they did not want him to see the gold.

Maurai knew that in his village the English did not allow Africans to possess gold—but to the whites it was something very precious. They were always talking about it, always counting it and wrapping it and sending it away by boat, or receiving it from England.

If a black boy stole a coin of gold, they would give him a great many years in prison to think about it. This Maurai knew. And suddenly he thought, looking at his own small hands, "Maybe that's why the black people hate me, because I am the color of gold."

Just then his father came out of his office and handed him the letter. "Here, Maurai, take this note to Captain Higgins of the *Drury* and tell him I shall expect him for tea at four."

"Yes, sir," said Maurai as he went out into the native street and down toward the river where the masts of the big boat towered.

On the dock everyone was busy. There were women selling things to eat and boys waiting for sailors to come ashore. Winches rattled, and the cranes lifted up their loads of palm oil and cocoa beans. Ebony-black men, naked to the waist, the sweat pouring off them, loaded the rope hampers before they swung up and over and down into the dark hole of the big ship. Their sweat fell from shining black bodies onto the bags of cocoa beans and went away to England and came back in gold for the white men to count in banks as though it were the most precious thing in the world.

Maurai went up the steep swinging stairway at the side of the ship, past the sailors leaning over the deck rail, and on up to the bridge and the captain's office. The captain took the letter from the little golden boy without a word.

As Maurai descended from the bridge he could see directly down into the great dark holes where went the palm oil and the cocoa beans, and where more sweating ebony-black men were stowing away the cargo for its trip to England.

One of the white sailors grabbed Maurai on the well deck and asked, "You take me see one fine girl?" because he naturally thought Maurai was one of the many little boys who are regularly sent to the dock on Steamer Days by the prostitutes, knowing only one or two vile phrases in English and the path to the prostitute's door. The sailors fling them a penny, perhaps, if they happen to like the black girls to whom the child leads them.

"I am not a guide boy," said Maurai, as he pulled away from the sailor and went on down the swinging stairs to the dock. There the boys who were runners for the girls in the palm huts laughed and made fun of this little youngster who was neither white nor black. They called him

an ugly yellow name. And Maurai turned and struck one
of the boys in the face.

But they did not fight fair, these dock boys. A dozen
of them began to strike and kick at Maurai, and even the
black women squatting on the wharf selling fruits and
sweetmeats got up and joined the boys in their attack,
while the sailors leaning on the rail of the English steamer
had great fun watching the excitement.

The little black boys ran Maurai away from the wharf
in a trail of hooting laughter. In the wide grassy street he
wiped the blood from his nose and looked down at his white
shirt, torn and grimy from the blows of the wharf rats. He
thought how, even in his English clothes, a sailor had taken
him for a prostitute's boy and had asked him to find "one
fine girl" for him.

The little mulatto youngster went slowly up the main
street past the bank where his father worked, past the
house of the man who sells parrots and monkeys to the sailors, on past the big bayamo tree where the vendors of
palm wine have their stands, on to the very edge of town
—which is the edge of the jungle, too—and down a narrow
path through a sudden tangle of vines and flowers, until he
came to a place where the still backwaters of the lagoon
formed a pool on whose grassy banks the feet of the obeah
dancers dance in nights of moon.

Here Maurai took off his clothes and went into the water, cool to his bruised little body. He swam well, and he
was not afraid of snakes or crocodiles. He was not afraid of
anything but white people and black people—and gold.
Why, he wondered in the water, was his body the color of
gold? Why wasn't he black or white—like his mother or
like his father, one or the other—but not just (he remembered that ugly word of the wharf rats) a *bastard* of gold?

Filling his lungs with air and holding his breath, down, down, Maurai went, letting his naked body touch the cool muddy bottom of the deep lagoon.

"Suppose I were to stay here forever," he thought, "in the dark, at the bottom of this pool?"

But, against his will, his body shot upward like a cork and his skin caught the sun in the middle of the big pool, and he kept on swimming around and around, loath to go back to the house in the enclosure where his father would soon be having the white captain to tea in the living room, but where he, Maurai, and the little dark girl with whom his father slept, would, of course, eat in the kitchen.

But since he had begun to be awfully hungry and awfully tired, he came out of the water to lie down on the grassy bank and dry in the sun. And probably because he was only twelve years old, Maurai began to cry. He thought about his mother who was dead and his father who would eventually retire and go back to England, leaving him in Africa—where nobody wanted him.

Out of the jungle two bright birds came flying and stopped to sing in a tree above his head. They did not know that a little boy was crying on the ground below them. They paid no attention to the strange sounds that came from that small golden body on the bank of the lagoon. They simply sang a moment, flashed their bright wings, and flew away.

Pushcart Man

● *THE* usual Saturday night squalls and brawls were taking place as the Push-cart Man trucked up Eighth Avenue in Harlem. A couple walking straggle-legged

21

got into a fight. A woman came to take her husband home from the corner saloon but he didn't want to go. A man said he had paid for the last round of drinks. The bartender said he hadn't. The squad car came by. A midget stabbed a full-grown man. Saturday night jumped.

"Forgive them, Father, for they know not what they do," said a Sanctified Sister passing through a group of sinners.

"Yes, they do know what they do," said a young punk, "but they don't give a damn!"

"Son, you oughtn't to use such language!"

"If you can't get potatoes, buy tomatoes," yelled the Pushcart Man. "Last call! Pushing this cart on home!"

"Have you got the *Times*?" asked a studious young man at a newsstand where everybody was buying the *Daily News*.

"I got the *News* or *Mirror*," said the vendor.

"No," said the young man, "I want the *Times*."

"You can't call my mother names and live with me," said a dark young fellow to a light young girl.

"I did not call your mother a name," said the girl. "I called *you* one."

"You called *me* a son of a—"

"Such language!" said the Sanctified Sister.

"He just ain't no good," explained the girl. "Spent half his money already and ain't brought home a thing to eat for Sunday."

"Help the blind, please," begged a kid cup-shaker pushing a blind man ahead of him.

"That man ain't no more blind than me," declared a fellow in a plaid sport shirt.

"I once knew a blind man who made more money begging than I did working," said a guy leaning on a mailbox.

"You didn't work very hard," said the Sport Shirt. "I

never knowed you to keep a job more than two weeks straight. Hey, Mary, where you going?"

"Down to the store to get a pint of ice cream." A passing girl paused. "My mama's prostrate with the heat."

An old gentleman whose eyes followed a fat dame in slacks muttered, "Her backside looks like a keg of ale."

"It's a shame," affirmed a middle-aged shopper on her way in the chicken store, "slacks and no figure."

"If you don't like pomatoes, buy totatoes!" cried the Pushcart Man.

"This bakery sure do make nice cakes," said a little woman to nobody in particular, "but they's so high."

"Don't hit me!" yelled a man facing danger, in the form of two fists.

"Stop backing up!"

"Then stop coming forward—else I'll hurt you." He was cornered. A crowd gathered.

"You children go on home," chided a portly matron to a flock of youngsters. "Fights ain't for children."

"You ain't none of my mama."

"I'm glad I ain't."

"And we don't have to go home."

"You-all ought to be in bed long ago! Here it is midnight!"

"There ain't nobody at my house."

"You'd be home if I was any relation to you," said the portly lady.

"I'm glad you ain't."

"Hit me! Just go on and hit me—and I'll cut you every way there is," said the man.

"I ain't gonna fight you with my bare fists cause you ain't worth it."

"Break it up! Break it up! Break it up!" barked the cop. They broke it up.

"Let's go play in 143rd Street," said a little bowlegged boy. "There's blocks of ice down there we can sit on and cool off."

"If you don't get potatoes, buy tomatoes," cried the Pushcart Man.

A child accidentally dropped a pint of milk on the curb as he passed. The child began to cry.

"When you get older," the Pushcart Man consoled the child, "you'll be glad it wasn't Carstairs you broke. Here's a dime. Buy some more milk. I got tomatoes, potatoes," cried the pushcart vendor. "Come and get 'em—'cause I'm trucking home."

● *Why, You Reckon?*

● *WELL*, sir, I ain't never been mixed up in nothin' wrong before nor since and I don't intend to be again, but I was hongry that night. Indeed, I was! Depression times before the war plants opened up.

I was goin' down a Hundred Thirty-third Street in the snow when another colored fellow what looks hongry sidetracks me and says, "Say, buddy, you wanta make a little jack?"

"Sure," I says. "How?"

"Stickin' up a guy," he says. "The first white guy what comes out o' one o' these speak-easies and looks like bucks, we gonna grab him!"

"Oh, no," says I.

"Oh, yes, we will," says this other guy. "Man, ain't you hongry? Didn't I see you down there at the charities today, not gettin' nothin'—like me? You didn't get a thing, did you? Hell, no! Well, you gotta take what you want, that's all, reach out and *take* it," he says. "Even if you are starvin', don't starve like a fool. You must be in love with white folks, or somethin'. Else scared. Do you think they care anything about you?"

"No," I says.

"They sure don't," he says. "These here rich folks comes up to Harlem spendin' forty or fifty bucks in the night clubs and speak-easies and don't care nothin' 'bout you and me out here in the street, do they? Huh? Well, one of 'em's gonna give up some money tonight before he gets home."

"What about the cops?"

"To hell with the cops!" said the other guy. "Now, listen, now. I live right here, sleep on the ash pile back of the furnace down in this basement. Don't nobody never come down there after dark. They let me stay here for keepin' the furnace goin' at night. It's kind of a fast house upstairs, you understand. Now, you grab this here guy we pick out, push him down to the basement door, right here, I'll pull him in, we'll drag him on back yonder to the furnace room and rob him, money, watch, clothes, and all. Then push him out in the rear court. If he hollers—and he sure will holler when that cold air hits him—folks'll just think he's some drunken white man what's fell out with some chocolate baby upstairs and has had to run and leave his clothes behind him. But by that time we'll be long gone. What do you say, boy?"

Well, sir, I'm tellin' you, I was so tired and hongry and cold that night I didn't hardly know what to say, so I said all right, and we decided to do it. Looked like to me 'bout that time a Hundred Thirty-third Street was just workin' with people, taxis cruisin', women hustlin', white folks from downtown lookin' for hot spots.

It were just midnight.

This guy's front basement door was right near the door of the Dixie Bar where that woman sings the kind of blues ofays is crazy about.

Well, sir! Just what we wanted to happen happened right off. A big party of white folks in furs and things come down the street. They musta parked their car on Lenox, 'cause they wasn't in no taxi. They was walkin' in the snow. And just when they got right by us one o' them white women says "Ed-*ward*," she said, "Oh, darlin', don't you know I left my purse and cigarettes and compact in the car. Please go and ask the chauffeur to give 'em to you." And they went on in the Dixie. The boy started toward Lenox again.

Well, sir, Edward never did get back no more that evenin' to the Dixie Bar. No, pal, uh-hum! 'Cause we nabbed him. When he come back down the street in his evenin' clothes and all, with a swell black overcoat on that I wished I had, just a-tippin' so as not to slip up and fall on the snow, I grabbed him. Before he could say Jack Robinson, I pulled him down the steps to the basement door, the other fellow jerked him in, and by the time he knew where he was, we had that white boy back yonder behind the furnace in the coalbin.

"Don't you holler," I said on the way down.

There wasn't much light back there, just the raw gas comin' out of a jet, kind of blue-like, blinkin' in the coal dust. Took a few minutes before we could see what he looked like.

"Ed-*ward*," the other fellow said, "don't you holler in this coal bin."

But Edward didn't holler. He just sat down on the coal. I reckon he was scared weak-like.

"Don't you throw no coal neither," the other fellow said. But Edward didn't look like he was gonna throw coal.

"What do you want?" he asked by and by in a nice white-folks kind of voice. "Am I kidnaped?"

Well, sir, we never thought of kidnapin'. I reckon we both looked puzzled. I could see the other guy thinkin' maybe we *ought* to hold him for ransom. Then he musta decided that that weren't wise, 'cause he says to this white boy, "No, you ain't kidnaped," he says. "We ain't got no time for that. We's hongry right *now*, so, buddy, gimme your money."

The white boy handed out of his coat pocket amongst other things a lady's pretty white beaded bag that he'd been sent after. My partner held it up.

"Doggone," he said, "my gal could go for this. She likes purty things. Stand up and lemme see what else you got."

The white guy got up and the other fellow went through his pockets. He took out a wallet and a gold watch and a cigarette lighter, and he got a swell key ring and some other little things colored folks never use.

"Thank you," said the other guy, when he got through

friskin' the white boy, "I guess I'll eat tomorrow! And smoke right now," he said, opening up the white boy's cigarette case. "Have one," and he passed them swell fags around to me and the white boy, too. "What kind is these?" he wanted to know.

"Benson's Hedges," said the white boy, kinder scared-like, 'cause the other fellow was makin' an awful face over the cigarette.

"Well, I don't like 'em," the other fellow said, frownin' up. "Why don't you smoke decent cigarettes? Where do you get off, anyhow?" he said to the white boy standin' there in the coalbin. "Where do you get off comin' up here to Harlem with these kind of cigarettes? Don't you know no colored folks smoke these kind of cigarettes? And what're you doin' bringin' a lot of purty rich women up here wearin' white fur coats? Don't you know it's more'n we colored folks can do to get a black fur coat, let alone a white one? I'm askin' you a question," the other fellow said.

The poor white fellow looked like he was gonna cry. "Don't you know," the colored fellow went on, "that I been walkin' up and down Lenox Avenue for three or four months tryin' to find some way to earn money to get my shoes half-soled? Here, look at 'em." He held up the palms of his feet for the white boy to see. There were sure big holes in his shoes. "Looka here!" he said to that white boy. "Still you got the nerve to come up here to Harlem all dressed up in a tuxedo suit with a stiff shirt on and diamonds shinin' out of the front of it, and a silk muffler on and a big heavy overcoat! Gimme that overcoat," the other fellow said.

He grabbed the white guy and took off his overcoat.

"We can't use that M.C. outfit you got on," he said, talk-

ing about the tux. "But we might be able to make earrings
for our janes out of them studs. Take 'em off," he said to
the white kid.

All this time I was just standin' there, wasn't doin'
nothin'. The other fellow had taken all the stuff, so far,
and had his arms full.

"Wearin' diamonds up here to Harlem, and me starvin'!"
the other fellow said. "Goddamn!"

"I'm sorry," said the white fellow.

"Sorry?" said the other guy. "What's your name?"

"Edward Peedee McGill, III," said the white fellow.

"What third?" said the colored fellow. "Where's the
other two?"

"My father and grandfather," said the white boy. "I'm
the third."

"I had a father and a grandfather, too," said the other
fellow, "but I ain't no third. I'm the first. Ain't never been
one like me. I'm a new model." He laughed out loud.

When he laughed, the white boy looked real scared. He
looked like he wanted to holler. He sat down in the coal
agin. The front of his shirt was all black where he took the
diamonds out. The wind came in through a broken pane
above the coalbin and the white fellow sat there shiverin'.
He was just a kid—eighteen or twenty maybe—runnin'
around to night clubs.

"We ain't gonna kill you," the other fellow kept
laughin'. "We ain't got the time. But if you sit in that coal
long enough, white boy, you'll be black as me. Gimme your
shoes. I might maybe can sell 'em."

The white fellow took off his shoes. As he handed them
to the colored fellow, he had to laugh, hisself. It looked so
crazy handin' somebody else your shoes. We all laughed.

"But I'm laughin' last," said the other fellow. "You two

can stay here and laugh if you want to, both of you, but I'm gone. So long!"

And, man, don't you know he went on out from that basement and took all that stuff! Left me standin' just as empty-handed as when I come in there. Yes, sir! He left me with that white boy standin' in the coal. He'd done took the money, the diamonds, and everythin', even the shoes! And me with nothin'! Was I stung? I'm askin' you!

"Ain't you gonna gimme none?" I hollered, runnin' after him down the dark hall. "Where's my part?"

I couldn't even see him in the dark—but I *heard* him.

"Get back there," he yelled at me, "and watch that white boy till I get out o' here. Get back there," he hollered, "or I'll knock your livin' gizzard out! I don't know you."

I got back. And there me and that white boy was standin' in a strange coalbin, him lookin' like a picked chicken—and me *feelin'* like a fool. Well, sir, we both had to laugh again.

"Say," said the white boy, "is he gone?"

"He ain't here," I said.

"Gee, this was exciting," said the white fellow, turning up his tux collar. "This was thrilling!"

"What?" I says.

"This is the first exciting thing that's ever happened to me," said the white guy. "This is the first time in my life I've ever had a good time in Harlem. Everything else has been fake, a show. You know, something you pay for. This was real."

"Say, buddy," I says, "if I had your money, I'd be always having a good time."

"No, you wouldn't," said the white boy.

"Yes, I would, too," I said, but the white boy shook his

head. Then he asked me if he could go home, and I said, "Sure! Why not?" So we went up the dark hall. I said, "Wait a minute."

I went up and looked, but there wasn't no cops or nobody much in the streets, so I said, "So long," to that white boy. "I'm glad you had a good time." And left him standin' on the sidewalk in his stocking feet waitin' for a taxi.

I went on up the street hongrier than I am now. And I kept thinkin' about that boy with all his money. I said to myself, "What do you suppose is the matter with rich white folks? Why you reckon they ain't happy?"

● *Saratoga Rain*

● *THE* wind blew. Rain swept over the roof. Upstairs the man and woman lay close together. He held her in his arms, drowsily, sleepily, head half buried in the covers, the scent of bodies between them. The rain came down.

She said, "Ben, I love you." To her, thirty years of muddy yesterdays were as nothing.

He said, "I like you, too, babe." And all the dice on all the tables from Reno to Saratoga were forgotten.

It was early morning. The rain came down. They didn't care. They were together in the darkened room, heads half buried in the covers. They had each other. They didn't remember now the many cliffs they'd had to climb nor the lurking tomorrows of marsh and danger.

They would never be angels and have wings—that they knew for sure. But at the moment they had each other.

That moment, that rainy morning, not even that whole day would last very long. Indeed, it might never repeat itself. Things had a way of moving swiftly with each of them, leaving memories, raising scars, and passing on. But they did not choose to remember now the aching loneliness of time, warm in bed as they were, with the rain falling outside.

They did not choose to remember (for her) the stable boy who had been her lover last night, nor the jockey who had been so generous with his money the week before but had fallen yesterday in the steeple chase, lost his mount, and broken his neck.

They did not (for him) choose to remember the swift rattle of crooked dice in the fast fading game at the corner, the recollection of the startled look on that Florida simpleton's face when he saw his month's pay gone.

For neither of them now the memory of muddy water in the gutter of life, because on this early August morning the rain fell straight out of the sky—clean.

The room is pleasantly dark and warm, the house safe and, though neither of them will ever be angels with wings, at the moment they have each other.

"I like you," Ben said.

"I love you," she whispered.

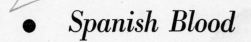

Spanish Blood

● *IN THAT* amazing city of Manhattan where people are forever building things anew, during prohibition times there lived a young Negro called Valerio Gutierrez whose mother was a Harlem laundress, but whose father was a Puerto Rican sailor. Valerio grew up in the streets. He was never much good at school, but he was swell at selling papers, pitching pennies, or shooting pool. In his teens he became one of the smoothest dancers in the Latin-American quarter north of Central Park. Long before the rhumba became popular, he knew how to do it in the real Cuban way that made all the girls afraid to dance with him. Besides, he was very good looking.

At seventeen, an elderly Chilean lady who owned a beauty parlor called La Flor began to buy his neckties. At eighteen, she kept him in pocket money and let him drive her car. At nineteen, younger and prettier women—a certain comely Spanish widow, also one Dr. Barrios' pale wife —began to see that he kept well dressed.

"You'll never amount to nothin'," Hattie, his brown-skinned mother said. "Why don't you get a job and work? It's that foreign blood in you, that's what it is. Just like your father."

"*Que va?*" Valerio replied, grinning.

"Don't you speak Spanish to me," his mama said. "You know I don't understand it."

"O.K., mama," Valerio said, "*Yo voy a trabajar.*"

"You better *trabajar,*" his mama answered. "And I mean work, too! I'm tired o' comin' home every night from that Chinee laundry and findin' you gone to the dogs. I'm gonna move out o' this here Spanish neighborhood anyhow, way up into Harlem where some real *colored* people is, I mean American Negroes. There ain't nobody settin' a decent example for you down here 'mongst all these Cubans and Puerto Ricans and things. I don't care if your father was one of 'em, I never did like 'em real well."

"Aw, ma, why didn't you ever learn Spanish and stop talking like a spook?"

"Don't you spook me, you young hound, you! I won't stand it. Just because you're straight-haired and yellow and got that foreign blood in you, don't you spook me. I'm your mother and I won't stand for it. You hear me?"

"Yes, m'am. But you know what I mean. I mean stop talking like most colored folks—just because you're not white you don't have to get back in a corner and stay there. Can't we live nowhere else but way up in Harlem, for instance? Down here in 106th Street, white and colored families live in the same house—Spanish-speaking families, some white and some black. What do you want to move further up in Harlem for, where everybody's all black? Lots of my friends down here are Spanish and Italian, and we get along swell."

"That's just what I'm talkin' about," said his mother. "That's just why I'm gonna move. I can't keep track of you, runnin' around with a fast foreign crowd, all mixed up with every what-cha-ma-call-it, lettin' all shades o' women give you money. Besides, no matter where you move, or what language you speak, you're still colored less'n your skin is white."

"Well, I won't be," said Valerio, "I'm American, Latin-American."

"Huh!" said his mama. "It's just by luck that you even got good hair."

"What's that got to do with being American?"

"A mighty lot," said his mama, "in America."

They moved. They moved up to 143rd Street, in the very middle of "American" Harlem. There Hattie Gutierrez was happier—for in her youth her name had been

Jones, not Gutierrez, just plain colored Jones. She had come from Virginia, not Latin America. She had met the Puerto Rican seaman in Norfolk, had lived with him there and in New York for some ten or twelve years and borne him a son, meanwhile working hard to keep him and their house in style. Then one winter he just disappeared, probably missed his boat in some far-off port town, settled down with another woman, and went on dancing rhumbas and drinking rum without worry.

Valerio, whom Gutierrez left behind, was a handsome child, not quite as light as his father, but with olive-yellow skin and Spanish-black hair, more foreign than Negro. As he grew up, he became steadily taller and better looking. Most of his friends were Spanish-speaking, so he possessed their language as well as English. He was smart and amusing out of school. But he wouldn't work. That was what worried his mother, he just wouldn't work. The long hours and low wages most colored fellows received during depression times never appealed to him. He could live without struggling, so he did.

He liked to dance and play billiards. He hung out near the Cuban theater at 110th Street, around the pool halls and gambling places, in the taxi dance emporiums. He was all for getting the good things out of life. His mother's moving up to black 143rd Street didn't improve conditions any. Indeed, it just started the ball rolling faster, for here Valerio became what is known in Harlem as a big-timer, a young sport, a hep cat. In other words, a man-about-town.

His sleek-haired yellow star rose in a chocolate sky. He was seen at all the formal invitational affairs given by the exclusive clubs of Harlem's younger set, although he belonged to no clubs. He was seen at midnight shows stretching into the dawn. He was even asked to Florita Sutton's famous Thursday midnight-at-homes where visiting dukes, English authors, colored tap dancers, and dinner-coated downtowners vied for elbow room in her small Sugar Hill apartment. Hattie, Valerio's mama, still kept her job ironing in the Chinese laundry—but nobody bothered about his mama.

Valerio was a nice enough boy, though, about sharing his income with her, about pawning a ring or something someone would give him to help her out on the rent or the insurance policies. And maybe, once or twice a week, mama might see her son coming in as she went out in the morning or leaving as she came in at night, for Valerio often slept all day. And she would mutter, "The Lord knows, cause I don't, what will become of you, boy! You're just like your father!"

Then, strangely enough, one day Valerio got a job. A good job, too—at least, it paid him well. A friend of his ran an after-hours night club on upper St. Nicholas Avenue. Gangsters owned the place, but they let a Negro run it. They had a red-hot jazz band, a high-yellow revue, and bootleg liquor. When the Cuban music began to hit Harlem, they hired Valerio to introduce the rhumba. That was something he was really cut out to do, the rhumba. That wasn't work. Not at all, *hombre!* But it was a job, and his mama was glad.

Attired in a yellow silk shirt, white satin trousers, and a bright red sash, Valerio danced nightly to the throbbing drums and seed-filled rattles of the tropics—accompanied by the orchestra's usual instruments of joy. Valerio danced with a little brown Cuban girl in a red dress, Concha, whose hair was a mat of darkness and whose hips were nobody's business.

Their dance became the talk of the town—at least, of

that part of the town composed of night-lifers—for Valerio danced the rhumba as his father had taught him to dance it in Norfolk when he was ten years old, innocently—un-expurgated, happy, funny, but beautiful, too—like a gay, sweet longing for something that might be had, some time, maybe, some place or other.

Anyhow, business boomed. Ringside tables filled with people who came expressly to see Valerio dance.

"He's marvelous," gasped ladies who ate at the Ritz any time they wanted to.

"That boy can dance," said portly gentlemen with of-fices full of lawyers to keep track of their income tax. "He can dance!" And they wished they could, too.

"Hot stuff," said young rum-runners, smoking reefers and drinking gin—for these were prohibition days.

"A natural-born eastman," cried a tan-skin lady with a diamond wrist-watch. "He can have anything I got."

That was the trouble! Too many people felt that Valerio could have anything they had, so he lived on the fat of the land without making half an effort. He began to be invited to fashionable cocktail parties downtown. He often went out to dinner in the East 50's with white folks. But his mama still kept her job in the Chinese laundry.

Perhaps it was a good thing she did in view of what finally happened, for to Valerio the world was nothing but a swagger world tingling with lights, music, drinks, money, and people who had everything—or thought they had. Each night, at the club, the orchestra beat out its astounding songs, shook its rattles, fingered its drums. Valerio put on his satin trousers with the fiery red sash to dance with the little Cuban girl who always had a look of pleased surprise on her face, as though amazed to find dancing so good.

Somehow she and Valerio made their rhumba, for all their hip-shaking, clean as a summer sun.

Offers began to come in from other night clubs, and from small producers as well. "Wait for something big, kid," said the man who ran the cabaret. "Wait till the Winter Garden calls you."

Valerio waited. Meanwhile, a dark young rounder named Sonny, who wrote number bets for a living, had an idea for making money off of Valerio. They would open an apartment together where people could come after the night clubs closed—come and drink and dance—and love a little if they wanted to. The money would be made from the sale of drinks—charging very high prices to keep the riffraff out. With Valerio as host, a lot of good spenders would surely call. They could get rich.

"O.K. by me," said Valerio.

"I'll run the place," said Sonny, "and all you gotta do is just be there and dance a little, maybe—you know—and make people feel at home."

"O.K.," said Valerio.

"And we'll split the profit two ways—me and you."

"O.K."

So they got a big Seventh Avenue apartment, furnished it with deep, soft sofas and lots of little tables and a huge icebox and opened up. They paid off the police every week. They had good whisky. They sent out cards to a hundred downtown people who didn't care about money. They informed the best patrons of the cabaret where Valerio danced—the white folks who thrilled at becoming real Harlem initiates going home with Valerio.

From the opening night on, Valerio's flat filled with white people from midnight till the sun came up. Mostly a sporty crowd, young blades accompanied by ladies of the chorus, race-track gentlemen, white cabaret entertainers out for amusement after their own places closed, musical-comedy stars in search of new dance steps—and perhaps three or four brown-skin ladies-of-the-evening and a couple of chocolate gigolos, to add color.

There was a piano player. Valerio danced. There was impromptu entertaining by the guests. Often famous radio stars would get up and croon. Expensive night-club names might rise to do a number—or several numbers if they were tight enough. And sometimes it would be hard to stop them when they really got going.

Occasionally guests would get very drunk and stay all night, sleeping well into the day. Sometimes one might sleep with Valerio.

Shortly all Harlem began to talk about the big red roadster Valerio drove up and down Seventh Avenue. It was all nickel-plated—and a little blonde revue star known on two continents had given it to him, so folks said. Valerio was on his way to becoming a gigolo de luxe.

"That boy sure don't draw no color lines," Harlem commented. "No, sir!

"And why should he?" Harlem then asked itself rhetorically. "Colored folks ain't got no money—and money's what he's after, ain't it?"

But Harlem was wrong. Valerio seldom gave a thought to money—he was having too good a time. That's why it was well his mama kept her job in the Chinese laundry, for one day Sonny received a warning, "Close up that flat of yours, and close it damn quick!"

Gangsters!

"What the hell?" Sonny answered the racketeers. "We're payin' off, ain't we—you and the police, both? So what's wrong?"

"Close up, or we'll break you up," the warning came back. "We don't like the way you're running things, black boy. And tell Valerio to send that white chick's car back to her—and quick!"

"Aw, nuts!" said Sonny. "We're paying the police! You guys lay off."

But Sonny wasn't wise. He knew very well how little the police count when gangsters give orders, yet he kept right on. The profits had gone to his head. He didn't even tell Valerio they had been warned, for Sonny, who was trying to make enough money to start a number bank of his own, was afraid the boy might quit. Sonny should have known better.

One Sunday night about 3:30 A. M., the piano was going like mad. Fourteen couples packed the front room, dancing close and warm. There were at least a dozen folks whose names you'd know if you saw them in any paper, famous from Hollywood to Westport.

They were feeling good.

Sonny was busy at the door, and a brown bar-boy was collecting highball glasses, as Valerio came in from the club where he still worked. He went in the bedroom to change his dancing shoes for it was snowing and his feet were cold.

O, rock me, pretty mama, till the cows come home . . .

sang a sleek-haired Harlemite at the piano.

Rock me, rock me, baby, from night to morn . . .

when, just then, a crash like the wreck of the Hesperus resounded through the hall and shook the whole house as five Italian gentlemen in evening clothes who looked exactly like gangsters walked in. They had broken down the door.

Without a word they began to smash up the place with long axes each of them carried. Women began to scream, men to shout, and the piano vibrated, not from jazz-playing fingers, but from axes breaking its hidden heart.

"Lemme out," the piano player yelled. "Lemme out!" But there was panic at the door.

"I can't leave without my wrap," a woman cried. "Where is my wrap? Sonny, my ermine coat!"

"Don't move," one of the gangsters said to Sonny.

A big white fist flattened his brown nose.

"I ought to kill you," said a second gangster. "You was warned. Take this!"

Sonny spit out two teeth.

Crash went the axes on furniture and bar. Splintered glass flew, wood cracked. Guests fled, hatless and coatless. About that time the police arrived.

Strangely enough, the police, instead of helping protect the place from the gangsters, began themselves to break, not only the furniture, but also the *heads* of every Negro in sight. They started with Sonny. They laid the barman and the waiter low. They grabbed Valerio as he emerged from the bedroom. They beat his face to a pulp. They whacked the piano player twice across the buttocks. They had a grand time with their night sticks. Then they arrested all the colored fellows (and no whites) as the gangsters took their axes and left. That was the end of Valerio's apartment.

In jail Valerio learned that the woman who gave him the red roadster was being kept by a gangster who controlled prohibition's whole champagne racket and owned dozens of rum-running boats.

"No wonder!" said Sonny, through his bandages. "He got them guys to break up our place! He probably told the police to beat hell out of us, too!"

"Wonder how he knew she gave me that car?" asked Valerio innocently.

"White folks know everything," said Sonny.

"Aw, stop talking like a spook," said Valerio.

When he got out of jail, Valerio's face had a long night-stick scar across it that would never disappear. He still felt weak and sick and hungry. The gangsters had forbidden any of the night clubs to employ him again, so he went back home to mama.

"Umm-huh!" she told him. "Good thing I kept my job in that Chinee laundry. It's a good thing . . . Sit down and eat, son . . . What you gonna do now?"

"Start practicing dancing again. I got an offer to go to Brazil—a big club in Rio."

"Who's gonna pay your fare way down yonder to Brazil?"

"Concha," Valerio answered—the name of his Cuban rhumba partner whose hair was a mat of darkness. "Concha."

"A woman!" cried his mother. "I might a-knowed it! We're weak that way. My God, I don't know, boy! I don't know!"

"You don't know what?" asked Valerio, grinning.

"How women can help it," said his mama. "The Lord knows you're *just* like your father—and I took care o' him for ten years. I reckon it's that Spanish blood."

"*Que va!*" said Valerio.

Heaven to Hell

● *THERE* we was dancin' up the steps of glory, my husband, Mackenzie, and me, our earthly troubles over, when who should we meet comin' down but Nancy Smothers!

"That hussy!" I said, "how did she get up here?"

She had her white wings all folded around her, lookin' just like an Easter lily, 'cept that her face was chocolate.

"Nancy Smothers, if you come a-near my husband, I'm gonna crown you!" I said, "I done stood enough from you down on earth, let alone meetin' you in heaven."

All this while, Mackenzie ain't said a word. Shame! He knowed he's done wrong with that woman. Mackenzie lifted up his wings like as if he was gonna fly, but I dared him!

"Don't you lift a feather, you dog, you! Just hold your horses! I'm gonna ask God how come this Harlem hussy got to heaven anyhow."

Mackenzie and I went on up the golden stairs. I could see him strainin' his eyeballs, tryin' to look back without turning his head.

Nancy Smothers switched on down the steps, I reckon.

But I never did find out how she got in heaven—because just then I come out from under the ether.

I looked up and saw a pretty white nurse standin' there by my bed just like a angel. I hollered, "Where is Mackenzie? Was he hurt much, too? You know, he was drivin' when we hit that pole!"

The nurse said, "Don't worry, madam. Your husband's alright. He just got a broken arm when the car turned over. But he'll be in to see you by and by. They're keepin' him in the Men's Ward overnight."

"I'm glad he's safe," I said, "I sure am glad!"

Then the nurse said, "This lady's been here with you a long time, sitting by your bed. An old friend of yours, she says. She brought you some flowers."

So I turned my eyes—and there sat Nancy Smothers, right beside of my bed! Just as long-faced and hypocritical as she could be!

"Nancy," I said, "where am I—in heaven *or in hell?*"

"You's still on earth, Amelia," Nancy said sweetly, "and, honey, I just come from the Men's Ward where I seen Mackenzie. He says to tell you he's doin' well."

Even with three broken ribs I would have tried to kill Nancy—that hussy, bringing me messages from my own Mackenzie—but there was that nice white nurse standing beside me like an angel, and I always did hate to act up in front of white folks.

All I said was, "Nancy, I wish you'd been with us in that wreck! Then I could a-got some pleasure out of it. I'd just love to see you all crippled up."

"Shss-ss-s!" said the nurse. "You're weak! You mustn't talk so loud!"

"You shouldn't excite yourself, dear," said Nancy, rising, "so I'll be going on home. I know you're out of your head."

"I wish you'd go to . . ."

"Shss-sss-s-s!" said the nurse.

Then I realized I was startin' to act up in front of that nice, sweet white nurse, so I tried to smile. "Good-by, Nancy."

She said, "Good-by, Amelia," her eyes gleamin' like a chess-cat's. That snake! Snake!

When the nurse took my temperature again, she said, "That's strange, madam! Your fever's gone away up!"

"Strange, nothin'," I thought to myself.

But then how could that pretty young nurse know I was layin' there worryin' myself to death about whether Nancy Smothers went on home or not—*or if the hussy went back in the Men's Ward to set beside Mackenzie?*

Love can be worse than hell.

Sailor Ashore

"*WHAT'S* your story, Morning Glory?"

"Like your tail, Nightingale."

Azora answered the sailor with as impudent a couplet as she could muster on short notice. This rhymed jive was intended as a compliment, for the sailor was big, brown, and handsome, except that he had sad eyes. Azora was coffee-and-cream colored, leaning slightly to the heavy side.

The sailor took her in with his eyes and decided she would do. Their stools were side by side. The bar was cozy. He was just a little drunk.

"Hold your attitude," he said.

"Solid," affirmed Azora.

"Have a drink?"

"What you think?"

"Well, all reet! That's down my street! Name it!"

"White Horse. Send it trotting!"

"Get a commission?"

"Sure," said Azora. She thought she might as well tell the truth. This bird was probably hep anyhow. But that shouldn't keep him from spending money. Shore leave was short and gay spots scarce after midnight. Colored folks didn't have many after-hour places to go on Central Avenue for, with elections coming, the politicians were cleaning up the city.

"Yes," said Azora, "I get a commission. What's it to you?"

"Set her up," said the sailor to the bartender. "And gimme a gin. What's your name, Miss Fine Brown Frame?"

"Azora."

"Mine's Bill."

"Bill, how are you?"

"Like a ship left to drift. I been looking for you all night. Shall we drink some more here—or go to your house?"

"My house? You act like you know me."

"I feel like I know you. Where's the liquor store?"

"Two doors down, bootleg, extra charge."

"Let's dig it."

Outside the moon was brighter than the street lights, the stars big in the sky. The girl put her arm through Bill's.

"I don't live far," Azora said.

"I'll keep up with you."

"I'm fast as greased lightning and slippery as a pig," jived Azora. "Play my name and you liable to catch a gig."

"Ain't you from Chicago?" asked the sailor.

"Thirty-ninth and State," said Azora.

"I knowed it. All they do in Chicago's play policy. But out here on the Coast the Chinaman's got everything sewed up."

"Tight as Dick's hatband."

"If you beat that Chinese lottery with all them spots to mark—you really beat something," commented the sailor.

The lights in the liquor joint were hard as tin. "What kind of whisky you like, Azora, when you ain't boosting bar sales?"

"Any kind, honey."

They bought a pint and started home to her room. Away from the bright lights of the bar, in the cool night air, the sailor suddenly fell silent. Under the street lights Azora noticed that his face, when he wasn't talking or smiling, was very sad. Well, sometimes she felt sad, too, but she tried not to look it.

She lived in one of those little two-room boxes that sit back in yards in Los Angeles behind two or three more little houses. It was cozy inside. She turned the radio on and got out her tray of glasses. They drank. But the sailor remained quiet. He looked into the brown whisky as if he was looking for something. Maybe he is drunk, Azora thought, or just sleepy. He kept looking down, frowning.

"Why don't you look at me?" Azora asked.

"I don't see no crystal ball in your eyes," the sailor answered.

"Crystal ball?"

"Yah, I'm trying to see my future."

"What old future?"

"My black future."

"What about mine, honey?"

"Yours is sewed up," said the sailor.

"Sewed up?"

"Sure, you ain't gonna be nothing. Neither am I."

"Honey, what makes you talk so serious? We come here to have some fun," said the woman.

"We're colored, ain't we?"

"Sure! Colored as we can be."

"Then we can't get nowhere in this white man's country," said the sailor.

"Yes, we can, too. There ain't no use talking like that, baby. I got a little boy and I'm sure gonna make something out of him."

"I ain't talking about your little boy, Azora. I'm talking about you and me. We ain't gonna be nothing."

"You're something now, honey—a big, strong, fine stud." She leaned toward him. "What does them stripes mean on your arm?"

"Nothing. A colored sailor can have all the stripes he wants on his arm. The white man still cusses him out."

"Who cussed you out, honey? You had trouble on your ship today? Is that why, all a sudden, you so grouchy?"

"Yah, I had trouble. Looks like they think I'm a dog to 'buse around."

"Well, let's not talk about it no more. Leave your troubles aboard."

"Suppose I do leave 'em aboard? I run into 'em all over again ashore," he muttered. "Look how far from the docks *I* have to come to have a little fun. Can't even get a decent drink out at the port. The bars won't serve Negroes."

"Boy, you talk like you just now finding out you're colored. Now, me, I've been colored a long time."

"So've I, but—"

"But what?"

"I don't know. To listen at the radio you would think we never had no Jim Crow and lynchings and prejudice in America at all. Even the Southerners are talking about liberty and freedom. White folks is funny, Azora, especially when they get all noble and speechifying."

"True. But I can deal with 'em, can't you?"

"Naw, they get me in a squirrel cage."

"You take it too serious. I work for white folks every day, cook and scrub. It's hard work, too."

"Then what you doing out ballyhooing all night long?"

"Saturday, ain't it? Besides, suppose I hadn't been out, I wouldn't've run into you."

"You got something there! How old's your kid you mentioned?"

"Eleven. Sixth grade in school. He's a fine boy."

"Un-hum. Wish I had a kid."

"Never been married?"

"No." The sailor shook his head.

"I'm a grass widow. I got nobody either now. You reckon you and me could get along?"

"I been looking for a girl like you. Fix that last drink."

She mixed the whisky and soda.

"I've only got three months more to go in the navy."

"I've been on my job in Beverly Hills for ten years."

"No wonder you got such a sweet little shack. How come you've got no old man?"

"Colored men's all too much like you—got your mind on not being nothing. Always complaining, always discouraged. Always talking about this is a white man's world."

"This *is* a white man's world, ain't it?"

"No, it ain't! I'm in it, too! I'm colored—and I'm gonna make something out of my son."

"You always talking about your son. I'm talking about us now."

"There ain't no just us. There's us—and everybody else. If things is bad, change 'em! You a man, ain't you?"

"I hope so."

"Then talk like a man."

The sad look deepened in the sailor's eyes.

"You a mighty hard chick to get along with," he said.

"What did you ask me tonight when we first met in that bar?"

"I said, 'What's your story, Morning Glory?' " remembered the sailor.

"You've heard my tale, Nightingale," said the girl.

"The whisky is all gone," said the sailor. "I better go— seeing as how I ain't man enough for you."

He looked around for his cap, found it, and opened the door. Azora didn't try to stop him.

"Thanks for the inspiring conversation," he said as he closed the door.

He got a few steps down the path between the houses when he heard her knob turn. A rectangle of light fell into the yard with Azora's shadow silhouetted in the middle.

She called, "Say, listen, sailor! Wait a minute! Com'ere!"

Her voice was harder than before. He turned and saw

her standing in the doorway. Slowly he came back to the steps.

"Listen, sailor," said Azora, "ain't neither one of us gonna be nothing! I lied when I told you I had a son. I ain't got nobody. I don't work in Beverly Hills. I work on the streets and in bars. I ain't nothing but a hustler."

"I knowed what you was the minute I saw you," said the sailor.

"Yeah? Well, listen, kid! If I ever *did* have a son—and if I ever do have a job—if I wasn't what I am—I'd make something out of my son, if I had one! I swear to God I would, sailor!"

The man looked at the woman in the doorway a long time.

"I say, I swear to God I would," she repeated as he walked away.

● *Slice Him Down*

● *IN RENO* in the 30's, among the colored folks of the town, there were two main social classes—those who came to the city on a freight train and those who did not. The latter, or cushion-riders, were sometimes inclined to turn flat noses high at those who rode the rods by way of entry to the city. Supercilious glances on the part of old settlers and chair-car arrivals tobogganed down broad Negro noses at the black bums who like the white bums, both male and female, streamed through Nevada during the depression years on their way to or from the coast, to remain a while, if the law would let them, in THE BIGGEST LITTLE CITY IN THE WORLD—RENO—according to the official sign in electric lights near the station.

But, of course, the rod-riders got off nowhere near the station. If they were wise, bums from the East got off at Sparks, several miles from the famous mecca of unhappy wives, then they footed it into Reno. (Only passengers with tickets, coaches or Pullmans can afford the luxury of alighting directly at any station, anywhere.)

Terry and Sling came in one day on a fast freight from Salt Lake. Before that they had come from Cheyenne. And before that from Chicago—and then the line went South and got lost somewhere in a tangle of years and cotton fields and God-knows-what fantasies of blackness.

They were Southern shines. Sure, shines—darkies—niggers—Terry and Sling. At least, that's what the railroad bulls called them often enough on the road. And you don't deny anything to a railroad bull, do you? They hit too hard and shoot too fast. And, after all, why argue over a name? It's only when your belly's full and your pride's up that you want people to call you Mr. Terry, Mr. Sling . . . Mr. Man.

"What's your name, boy?" asked a colored voice in the near-darkness.

"What you care? You might be a detective."

Terry grinned from ear to ear at the compliment. He

put one hand in a raggedy, pocketless pocket and scratched himself.

"You's a no-name boy like me, heh, fella? Well, maybe you is equally as bad as me, too? Mean and hongry and bad! Listen, let's me and you travel together since we's on the road. What shall I call you?"

"Call me Sling."

Freights were being made up in the Chicago railroad yards at dusk. Rattlers on rollers going somewhere—must be better than here, Lawd, better than here.

"I'm tough, too," said Sling, eying a passing string of boxcars. "I eats pig iron for breakfast."

"Huh! I use cement for syrup on hot cakes made o' steel," said Terry.

"That's why I'm leavin' town," said scarred-up Sling, " 'cause I spit in a bozo's eye yesterday and killed him stone dead! I spit bullets."

Just then they grabbed a Westbound freight on the wing. They lied all the way to Omaha as they squatted in the corner of an open-lathed empty car where plenty of cattle had left plenty of smells on their various trips to the Chicago market.

"Why, man, I done killed me so many mens in my day that I'm scared I'll kill myself some time by accident," said Sling. "When I shaves myself, I tries not to look mean—to keep from pullin' my own razor across my own throat. I'm a bad jigaboo, son."

"Huh! You ain't nowheres near as bad as me," Terry lied, long tall lies, all the way from Omaha to Cheyenne. "Lemme tell you 'bout the last duster that crossed my path. He were an Al Capone—machine gun and all—and I just mowed him down with my little thirty-two on a forty-four frame. Man, I made lace curtains out of his a-nat-toe-mie!"

"Why?"

" 'Cause he were white, and I were mad 'cause he were messin' with my State Street gal."

"Man, you let women mess you up that way?"

"I did that time."

"They ain't worth fightin' about."

"I know it—but I does fight about 'em."

"I does, too, man, but I ain't gonna no mo'. I'm through fightin' 'bout women."

"Me, too."

"Then we's buddies. Womens done messed me up too much."

"And me."

By that time the coal car they were in was running too slow for anybody's good, nearing a town. What town? On the map, Cheyenne.

But no map ever made would have a dot on it for the alley where the garbage can was at the A-1 Café's back door that gave up only a half-dozen rinds of raw squash, a handful of bacon skins, and a few bread crusts to feed two long tall black boys named Terry and Sling.

"Let's get on down the road, boy." As the stars came out.

"Dust my broom, pal."

"Swing your feet, Terry. Let's make this early evenin' rattler."

> *Aw, do it freight train!*
> *Wheelers roll!*
> *Dog-gone my hard,*
> *Unlucky soul!*

Reno! The BIGGEST little CITY in the WORLD blazing its name in lights at night in a big arch of a sign all the way across the street. But they couldn't read the sign too

well. Hunger and rain and a bad education all stood between them and the reading of that sign.

Autumn in Reno! Dog-bite my onions! Stacks of shining
silver dollars on the tables—even in depression times—
wheels spinning in gambling places, folks winning, losing,
winning. THE BANK CLUB: big plate glass windows on
the main street. Stand right on the sidewalk and look in at
the Bank Club. Dice, keno, roulette, piles of silver. Pretty
sight.

"There must not be no law in Reno."

"Must ain't," said Sling.

"Must be all the cartwheels in the world in Reno."

"Must is," said Sling.

"Here we stays in Reno."

"Here we stays, Terry," said Sling.

As luck would have it, they got jobs, settled in Reno, got
a room, got gambling change, got girls. And there the trouble began—with the girls.

Terry was shining shoes at a stand in front of the station.
Sling was elbow-greasing the floor of a Chinese lottery and
dice joint, acting as general-janitor, bouncer, and errand
boy all in one. Between them, they made ten or twelve dollars a week, not bad in those times. Suits on credit—three
dollars down. Two-tone shoes. Near-silk shirts. Key chains
—without keys. Who cares about keys? You *wear* the
chains. String 'em across your breast! Hang 'em from your
pockets. Man, they shine like silver! Shine like gold—them
chains! You can't wear keys.

"Boy, you ought to see my gal! Three quarters cat—and
didn't come here on no freight train neither," said Terry,
putting a stocking cap on his head to make his hair lay
down.

"You come on a rattler, so hush," said Sling. "My gal did, too, so don't bring that up!"

"All right, pal! Take it easy! You know I'm a bad man."

"Almost as bad as I is, ain't you?" said Sling, spraying his armpits with rose-colored talcum from a tall ten-cent store box.

"You mean as bad as you would like to be," kidded Terry, at the same time wishing, in his heart of hearts, that he had a big knife scar somewhere on his body like the one Sling had halfway across his neck and down his shoulder blade—a true sign of battle. "You'd like to be tough," kidded Terry.

But Sling let that pass. He was kinda tired and in no mood for joking, nor quarreling, either. A Chinaman sure can work you hard in one day! Poor *hockaway* gets worked hard everywhere by everybody. Almost too tired to wash up and go see my gal. Dog-gone! That's why he used so much talcum powder, he was so tired.

Meanwhile, Terry put on his derby at a cocky angle, got that off his mind, and looked around under the bed for his shoes. As he tied his brown and white oxfords, he kept thinking in his mind how his sweet mama didn't come to Reno on no freight train. No, sir! Not that dame o' mine! Angelina Walls is her name, Mrs. Angelina Walls. Cooks for a white lady from Frisco who come to Reno to get unchained and brought along her maid. And the maid done fell for me! Ha! Ha! Angelina! Fell for a smooth black papa with a deep Chicago line. Old young Terry's done got himself a woman, sure enough.

"Boy, lend me your honey-brown tie, will you?"

"Aw-right," said Sling.

Tonight, Sling's thoughts were on his ladylove, too, tired as he was. Dark and Indian-looking, his particular girl. She didn't work much, neither. Just rested. She made her living—somehow. Wore a rabbit skin coat and a gold wrist-watch . . . Sure, she come to town on a freight train —but she rode in taxis on rainy nights! Had a nice room. Had a good heart. Liked an old long tall boy by the name of Sling, with a razor scar across his shoulder. Hot dog!

Her name was Charlie-Mae. Charlie-Mae what? I dunno! Nobody was ever heard to call her by her last name, if she had one. She might have had one, maybe. Who knows? Probably did. Charlie-Mae—Indian-looking girl in a rabbit skin coat with a gold wrist-watch, Lawd!

"Let's haul it to the club," said Terry, "soon's I go get Angelina."

"I'll pick you up," said Sling, "by and by. You truck on down."

So Terry tapped on down the street in his derby hat and honey-colored tie to get Mrs. Walls.

Shortly thereafter, in a sky-blue suit with wide shoulders, Sling went looking for Charlie-Mae, key chain just a-swinging, shining, and swinging.

Both boys really looked hot in the gorgeous sense—but the sad facts were that it was late November by now and neither one of them had yet worked up to an overcoat to cover their outer finery. So it should be recorded that before donning their stylish suits and ties and hats, they had put on underneath clean shirts various sweaters, sweat-shirts, and other warm but unsightly garments from their meager store in order the better to face the cold Nevada wind.

Saturday night in Reno. Back-alley Reno. Colored Reno by the railroad tracks where you can hear the trains go by. Where do they go, them trains? Where do they come from?

What is there where them trains go better than here, Lawd, better than here? Colored folks always live down by the railroad tracks, but is there any train anywhere runnin' where a man ain't black? Far or near, Lawd, is it better than here—Reno on a Saturday night?

"Anyhow, who gives a damn about being black, when he's hard and tough as I is?" said Terry, leaving the house near the park where he had called at the white lady's back door for his girl friend.

"Well, for a woman, it ain't easy being black," said Mrs. Angelina Walls. "I could a-been much better educated, had I been white. Now, down South where I growed up, there wasn't any schools hardly for colored. But as it were, I learned to read and write, and I holds my head high. I ain't common! I come here on a train, myself!"

"You all right with me," Terry said proudly as they walked down the street toward the alley where the colored club was located. "A high-toned woman like you's all right with me."

"Then don't mix me with no dirt," said Mrs. Angelina Walls. "That's one reason I don't like to go to this old club. Any-and-everybody goes there. Womens right off the street. Bums right off the freight."

"They sure do," said Terry, feeling kinda shamed to take her there, educated as she was. "But they ain't no place else for jigs to go in Reno."

"You right, honey," said Mrs. Angelina Walls. "We has to get a glass o' beer somewhere and dance a little bit once in a while."

"We sho' do."

"You can have a right smart good time at that there club," said Sling, as he and his girl came down the steps of the third-rate Japanese rooming house where she lived.

"We sho' can," said Charlie-Mae, buttoning her rabbit fur. "Um-m! This air smells good tonight."

"Would smell better if it weren't so cold," said Sling. "I never did like for winter to start coming."

"I do," said Charlie-Mae. "It's better for my business. I don't always have a nice affectionate fella like you to look after me."

"But you got me now," said Sling, "so you don't have to worry."

"When we gonna start living together?"

"Soon's I get my next pay from that Chinaman in the dice house. But I kinda hate to move away from Terry, 'cause me and him's been real good buddies. He's mighty nigh as bad a man as I is, and don't neither one of us take no foolishness. I'm tellin' you, Charlie-Mae," Sling lied, "you ought to seen how we used to do them railroad bulls when we was on the road together. We used to slice 'em right down! I mean, cut 'em to ribbons and leave their carcass in the railroad yard, if they messed with us."

"You did?"

"Sho' did."

"You and Terry?"

"Me and Terry! We used to slice them bulls right down."

"But Terry ain't got no scars."

"He sho' ain't," said Sling. "I just now thought o' that. I'm so bad, I done been scarred up two or three times, if not more."

"That's a lovely cut on your right shoulder," said Charlie-Mae. "But, say! Listen, not changing the subject, Terry's sure got a funny taste in women, ain't he? Going around with that old stuck-up yellow hussy they calls Mrs.

Angelina Walls. I heard her say she didn't speak to nobody what come here on a freight train, herself."

"She's got a high nose," said Sling. "But Terry, he's all right."

Packed and jammed, the club, on Saturday night. Little colored club in Reno. Six-foot bar and dance floor no bigger than a dime. Old piano with the front wide open, strings showing, and all the hammers of the notes bare, played by a little, fat, coal-black man in shirt sleeves with a glass of gin by his side. A young light-yellow boy beating drums out of this world!

Piano player singing as the dancers dance:

> *I'm goin' down de road and*
> *I won't look back a-tall.*
> *I say, Good-by, mama, it*
> *Ain't no use to call.*

> *I'm goin' down to Frisco and*
> *I'm goin' by myself.*
> *I'm sorry for you, honey, but*
> *You sho' Lawd will be left.*

Sling and Charlie-Mae dancing in a slow embrace. Mrs. Angelina Walls and Terry sitting at the bar drinking.

Angelina really shouldn't have had so many beers, with her education and reserve and all, but when you cook the whole week long for white folks over a hot stove, you need something on a Saturday night.

"A little recreation," she said, "a little recreation!"

"You right," said Terry, downing a straight whisky.

"Gimme another shetland," said Angelina. The barman drew a small glass of beer. "And don't you bother, baby," said Angelina, as Terry reached in his pocket to pay for it. "I make more money'n you do. I'll pay. Hurry up and drink your'n so you can have a glass or two on me."

"O.K.," said Terry, tipsy enough to begin mixing his drinks. "Gimme a shetland, too."

As the music ended, several of the dancers flocked toward the bar, among them Sling and Charlie-Mae, arm in arm.

"Here comes the common herd," said Angelina, but Terry didn't grasp what she said. Charlie-Mae heard, however—and understood, too—as she sat down on a stool and turned her back.

"Gimme two shetlands," Sling called to the barman. "Hy there, buddy," he said to Terry, slapping his pal on the back, "you's huggin' the rail mighty close tonight. Why don't you dance?"

But before Terry could answer, Mrs. Walls explained. "The floor at this club's too full of riffraff for me," she said. "I come here to Reno on a *train*, myself." She was aiming directly at Charlie-Mae sitting beside her.

"That's more'n your boy friend did," said Sling, grinning at Terry.

"Well, if he didn't," said Mrs. Walls in a high half-drunken voice, "he's a real man right on. He earns a decent living shining shoes—not working down in no Chinese rat hole like you, cleaning up after gamblers, and running around with womens what don't know they name."

Sling was shamed into silence—but Charlie-Mae whirled around toward Mrs. Walls and slapped her face. Angelina's beer went all over her dress. Terry pushed Charlie-Mae from her stool. She landed on the floor.

"Don't you touch my woman," Sling yelled at his pal.

"Well, tell her not to touch *my* woman, then," said

Terry. "Don't you know who I is? I'm badder'n usual to-night."

"Huh!" said Sling.

"Terry, protect me," Mrs. Walls cried, holding her well-slapped cheek. "A decent girl can't live in this town."

"No, they can't," said Charlie-Mae, rising, "not if they acts like you—and I'm around."

"Don't mess with her," warned Sling, glaring at Terry.

"Man, is you talking to me?" asked Terry of his friend.

"I'm bad," said Sling.

"Is you tryin' to tell *me* who's bad in this town? If there's anybody bad, it's Terry. I'm a terrible terrier this evenin', too!"

"Bark on!" said Sling.

"Listen, honey," pleaded Charlie-Mae loudly in Sling's ear, "do him like you said you did them railroad bulls—slice him down for knocking me off my stool."

Said Terry, "Slice who down?"

"Slice you down," said Sling, "if you fools around with me. You my buddy, and we don't want no trouble, but just leave me and Charlie-Mae alone, that's all, and take your old hinkty heifer out o' here where she belong, 'cause she can't stand no company sides herself. She's a fool!"

"Oh!" screamed Mrs. Walls. "You hear him, Terry? Hit him! Hit him for my sake!"

"If he do, he'll never hit another human," said Sling slowly.

"Boy," said Terry, "I'll pickle you in a minute in your own blood."

"And you'll be sliced baloney," said Sling.

"Not me!" cried Terry drawing a switch-blade and backing toward the wall. His knife was the kind that has a little button in it and double action. When you push the button once, the blade flies out halfway. When you push it twice, it flies out about six inches.

Switch-blades are dangerous weapons, but Sling was prepared. He drew a razor, a good old steel razor, slightly outmoded for shaving, but still useful for defense.

Didn't nobody holler, "Don't let 'em fight!"

On a Saturday night in a little club, down by the railroad track out West, in a town between the mountains, what could be more fun than a good fight with knives and razors? It didn't matter if they were buddies, them boys—didn't nobody holler, "Stop that fight!"

Women stood on stools and tables. The barman got on a beer keg behind the bar. The piano player brought his piano stool nearer the scene of combat.

Folks had to hold Charlie-Mae to keep her from attacking Angelina, for two fights at the same time would have spoilt the fun.

"You women wait," everybody said.

"Boy, I'm tellin' you, I mean business," warned Sling, his eyes red, his teeth shining, and his feelings hurt. "Don't come a-near me!"

"I done heard so much from you about how bad you is," said Terry. "I just want to see. You been my pal, but I believe you's lyin' about your badness."

His long face was a shiny oval under his derby. He was trembling.

"I'll cut you down," said Sling, "like you warn't no friend."

"Cut then—and don't talk," said Terry, " 'cause I'm quicker'n greased lightnin' and I'm liable to get you first."

Suddenly his knife flashed and Sling's left coat sleeve split like a torn ribbon—swiss-ss-sh! But at the same time Sling's razor made a moonlike upward movement and cut straight through the brim of Terry's derby, narrowly missing an eyebrow.

The crowd roared. It was getting good. Didn't nobody say, "Don't let them boys fight."

Sling, with a quick movement of his arm, sent the derby swirling through space and brought his weapon back into play for a slash at Terry's vitals, his flying razor cutting a wide gash straight across his friend's middle, slicing the front of Terry's pants open at the belt and exposing several layers of undergarments. But Terry's switch-blade went deep into Sling's fashionably padded shoulder before either stepped back.

Both began to bleed, but nobody fell. Their new and still unpaid-for suits got cut and stained. Blood dropped down on their two-tone shoes as the fighters stood apart, panting for a few moments.

A loud murmur went up from the crowd, and Mrs. Walls screamed, "My God!" as Sling's razor found the mark it had been looking for—a place where a cut would always show on a man so that people could say that he, Sling, had put it there. He slit the side of Terry's face right down, from temple to chin.

"Sling," Terry cried, "don't do that to me! Man, I'm bad! I'm telling you, I'm bad and I'll hurt you!"

"Lemme see," said Sling, panting against the bar, "I'se heard tell you's bad. Lemme see."

"I'll show you," said Terry, charging so swiftly that before Sling could sidestep, he ran his knife all the way up to the hilt in his companion's side—and left it there.

Sling looked down, saw where the knife had lodged, gasped, trembled, rolled his eyes up, and crumpled backward to the floor.

Terry saw his pal go down, taking the knife with him

embedded in his sky-blue coat, his mouth agape, his razor arm limp, his eyes like eggs. And something about the sight of that falling body made his own limbs begin to shake, his knees grow weaker, his bleeding jaw hurt more and more, and his throat fill up with his beating heart. Suddenly, he, too, passed out, sinking prone upon the floor.

"Here! Here! Here!" barked the bartender as he saw them both topple, "you two boys done fought enough now. Cut it out, I say! Cut it out!"

He jumped over the bar and pushed his way through the crowd. As Charlie-Mae shrieked hysterically and strong men turned their heads, the bartender stooped and pulled the knife from Sling's side.

"Funny," he said, frowning sharply, "there ain't no blood on this knife! Some of you-all take care o' Terry yonder while I see after this boy."

The bartender raised Sling up, but his unseeing head fell limply backward. Others crowded near to help and to stare. They took off his sky-blue coat. One arm was bloody. They took off his vest, too, and unbuttoned his lemon-cream shirt. Underneath, he had on a grey sweatshirt. They pulled that off. Under the sweatshirt he wore a ragged purple sweater. They removed that.

"I don't see how any knife ever got to his skin," said one of the helpers, "with all these clothes he's got on."

"I don't believe it did," said the bartender. "His side ain't bleedin'."

And sure enough, when they finally got down to Sling's cocoa-colored skin, he didn't have a scratch on his body—except that old scar across his shoulder. His arm was cut slightly, but his body proper was not harmed in the least.

"Pshaw! That there knife had to go through too many

wrappings. He ain't dead," said the bartender disappointedly.

"Boy, you wake up!"

He dropped Sling's head back on the floor with a bang, to turn his attention to Terry. By now, Terry was sitting up, a towel tied around his sliced slit cheek.

"Did I kill him?" Terry moaned. "Is I done kilt my partner?"

"Naw, you ain't killed nobody," the bartender barked. "Both you hucks get up off that floor and let things be as they were before this mess started. Shame on you, lettin' a little blood scare you—till you so weak you have to lay down. Sling, unroll them eyes!"

By this time, Sling's eyes were unrolled, and he felt his half-naked body in amazement at finding it still whole. Only his forearm bled a little where the fleshy part was cut. He sat up to look anxiously across at Terry.

Terry looked back at Sling and then pointed to his wounded jaw.

"Say, boy, is I got me a good scar?"

"Terry," Sling said, his voice shaking, "I thought I'd done killed you."

"I said, boy, is I got me a good scar?"

"Man," Sling said generously, "you got a better scar than I got now—'cause your'n is gonna be on your face where everybody can see it, and mine's just on my shoulder."

Terry grinned with delight. "All right, then," he said as he rose from the floor. "This fight's been *some* good after all! Get up from there, Sling, and put on your clothes. Let's have a drink."

As Sling gathered up his near-silk shirt and ragged

sweater, his well-sliced coat and wrinkled tie, Terry looked around for his "company."

"Where's my lady friend?" he asked.

"Who? Angelina Walls?" some woman answered. "Why, man, she runned out of here no sooner'n she seed you get cut! *She* couldn't be mixed up in no murder trial. She's too respectable."

"A hinkty hussy!" said Sling.

"She is for true," said Terry. "Come on, boy, let's drink."

Sling, his lemon-colored shirt tail out, looked around for his woman. "Charlie-Mae," he said, glaring at his erstwhile sweetie as she emerged all freshly powdered from the Ladies Room, "this boy's my pal, and here you done liked to made me kill him, right this evenin'. You get goin'!"

Charlie-Mae, heeding the look in Sling's eyes, got going. Without a word she donned her rabbit fur and left.

The two big fellows, tattered and torn, key chains dangling and sartorial effects awry, rested their elbows on the bar. They grinned proudly at one another.

"Two shetlands," Sling said to the bartender.

"For two bad men," said Terry, " 'cause we really bad!"

"We slice 'em down," said Sling.

"We really slice 'em down," said Terry.

● *Tain't So*

● *MISS LUCY CANNON* was **a** right nice old white woman, so Uncle Joe always stated, except that she really did *not* like colored folks, not even after she

77

come out West to California. She could never get over certain little Southern ways she had, and long as she knowed
my Uncle Joe, who hauled her ashes for her, she never
would call him *Mister*—nor any other colored man *Mister*
neither for that matter, not even the minister of the Bap-
tist Church who was a graduate of San Jose State College.
Miss Lucy Cannon just wouldn't call colored folks *Mister*
nor *Missus*, no matter who they was, neither in Alabama
nor in California.

She was always ailing around, too, sick with first one
thing and then another. Delicate, and ever so often she
would have a fainting spell, like all good Southern white
ladies. Looks like the older she got, the more she would be
sick and couldn't hardly get around—that is, until she went
to a healer and got cured.

And that is one of the funniest stories Uncle Joe ever
told me, how old Miss Cannon got cured of her heart and
hip in just one cure at the healer's.

Seems like for three years or more she could scarcely
walk—even with a cane—had a terrible bad pain in her
right leg from her knee up. And on her left side, her heart
was always just about to give out. She was in bad shape,
that old Southern lady, to be as spry as she was, always giving teas and dinners and working her colored help to
death.

Well, Uncle Joe says, one New Year's Day in Pasadena
a friend of hers, a Northern lady who was kinda old and
retired also and had come out to California to spend her
last days, too, and get rid of some parts of her big bank full
of money—this old lady told Miss Cannon, "Darling,
you just seem to suffer so all the time, and you say you've
tried all the doctors, and all kinds of baths and medicines.

Why don't you try my way of overcoming? Why don't you try faith?"

"Faith, honey?" says old Miss Lucy Cannon, sipping her jasmine tea.

"Yes, my dear," says the Northern white lady. "Faith! I have one of the best faith-healers in the world."

"Who is he?" asked Miss Lucy Cannon.

"She's a woman, dear," said old Miss Northern white lady. "And she heals by power. She lives in Hollywood."

"Give me her address," said Miss Lucy, "and I'll go to see her. How much do her treatments cost?"

Miss Lucy warn't so rich as some folks thought she was.

"Only Ten Dollars, dearest," said the other lady. "Ten Dollars a treatment. Go, and you'll come away cured."

"I have never believed in such things," said Miss Lucy, "nor disbelieved, either. But I will go and see." And before she could learn any more about the healer, some other friends came in and interrupted the conversation.

A few days later, however, Miss Lucy took herself all the way from Pasadena to Hollywood, put up for the week end with a friend of hers, and thought she would go to see the healer, which she did, come Monday morning early.

Using her customary cane and hobbling on her left leg, feeling a bit bad around the heart, and suffering terribly in her mind, she managed to walk slowly but with dignity a half-dozen blocks through the sunshine to the rather humble street in which was located the office and home of the healer.

In spite of the bright morning air and the good breakfast she had had, Miss Lucy (according to herself) felt pretty bad, racked with pains and crippled to the use of a cane.

When she got to the house she was seeking, a large frame dwelling, newly painted, she saw a sign thereon:

MISS PAULINE JONES

"So that's her name," thought Miss Lucy. "Pauline Jones, Miss Jones."

Ring And Enter said a little card above the bell. So Miss Lucy entered. But the first thing that set her back a bit was that nobody received her, so she just sat down to await Miss Jones, the healer who had, she heard, an enormous following in Hollywood. In fact, that's why she had come early, so she wouldn't have to wait long. Now, it was only nine o'clock. The office was open—but empty. So Miss Lucy simply waited. Ten minutes passed. Fifteen. Twenty. Finally she became all nervous and fluttery. Heart and limb! Pain, pain, pain! Not even a magazine to read.

"Oh, me!" she said impatiently, "What is this? Why, I never!"

There was a sign on the wall that read:

BELIEVE

"I will wait just ten minutes more," said Miss Lucy, glancing at her watch of platinum and pearls.

But before the ten minutes were up, another woman entered the front door and sat down. To Miss Lucy's horror, she was a colored woman! In fact, a big black colored woman!

Said Miss Lucy to herself, "I'll never in the world get used to the North. Now here's a great—my friend says great faith-healer, treating darkies! Why, down in Alabama, a Negro patient wouldn't dare come in here and sit down with white people like this!"

But, womanlike, (and having still five minutes to wait) Miss Lucy couldn't keep her mouth shut that long. She just had to talk, albeit to a Negro, so she began on her favorite subject—herself.

"I certainly feel bad this morning," she said to the colored woman, condescending to open the conversation.

"Tain't so," answered the Negro woman placidly—which sort of took Miss Lucy back a bit. She lifted her chin.

"Indeed, it is so," said she indignantly. "My heart is just about to give out. My breath is short."

"Tain't so a-tall," commented the colored woman.

"Why!" gasped Miss Lucy, "such impudence! I tell you *it is so!* I could hardly get down here this morning."

"Tain't so," said the Negro calmly.

"Besides my heart," went on Miss Lucy, "my right hip pains me so I can hardly sit here."

"I say, tain't so."

"I tell you it *is* so," screamed Miss Lucy. "Where is the healer? I won't sit here and suffer this—this impudence. I can't! It'll kill me! It's outrageous."

"Tain't so," said the large black woman serenely, whereupon Miss Lucy rose. Her pale face flushed a violent red.

"Where is the healer?" she cried, looking around the room.

"Right here," said the colored woman.

"What?" cried Miss Lucy. "You're the—why—you?"

"I'm Miss Jones."

"Why, I never heard the like," gasped Miss Lucy. "A *colored* woman as famous as you? Why, you must be lying!"

"Tain't so," said the woman calmly.

"Well, I shan't stay another minute," cried Miss Lucy.

"Ten Dollars, then," said the colored woman. "You've had your treatment, anyhow."

"Ten Dollars! That's entirely too much!"

"Tain't so."

Angrily Miss Lucy opened her pocketbook, threw a Ten Dollar bill on the table, took a deep breath, and bounced out. She went three blocks up Sunset Boulevard walking like the wind, conversing with herself.

" 'Tain't so,' " she muttered. " 'Tain't so!' I tell her I'm sick and she says, 'Tain't so!' "

On she went at a rapid gait, stepping like a young girl —so mad she had forgotten all about her infirmities, even her heart—when suddenly she cried, "Lord, have mercy, my cane! For the first time in three years, I'm *without* a cane!"

Then she realized that her breath was giving her no trouble at all. Neither was her leg. Her temper mellowed. The sunshine was sweet and warm. She felt good.

"Colored folks do have some funny kind of supernatural conjuring powers, I reckon," she said smiling to herself. Immediately her face went grim again. "But the impudence of 'em! Soon's they get up North—calling herself *Miss* Pauline Jones. The idea! Putting on airs and charging me Ten Dollars for a handful of *Tain't so's!*"

In her mind she clearly heard, "Tain't so!"

● One Friday Morning

● *THE* thrilling news did not come directly to Nancy Lee, but it came in little indirections that finally added themselves up to one tremendous fact: she had won the prize! But being a calm and quiet young lady, she did not say anything, although the whole high school buzzed with rumors, guesses, reportedly authentic announcements on the part of students who had no right to be making announcements at all—since no student really knew yet who had won this year's art scholarship.

But Nancy Lee's drawing was so good, her lines so sure, her colors so bright and harmonious, that certainly no other student in the senior art class at George Washington High was thought to have very much of a chance. Yet you never could tell. Last year nobody had expected Joe Williams to win the Artist Club scholarship with that funny modernistic water color he had done of the high-level bridge. In fact, it was hard to make out there was a bridge until you had looked at the picture a long time. Still, Joe Williams got the prize, was feted by the community's leading painters, club women, and society folks at a big banquet at the Park-Rose Hotel, and was now an award student at the Art School—the city's only art school.

Nancy Lee Johnson was a colored girl, a few years out of the South. But seldom did her high-school classmates think of her as colored. She was smart, pretty and brown, and fitted in well with the life of the school. She stood high in scholarship, played a swell game of basketball, had taken part in the senior musical in a soft, velvety voice, and had never seemed to intrude or stand out except in pleasant ways, so it was seldom even mentioned—her color.

Nancy Lee sometimes forgot she was colored herself. She liked her classmates and her school. Particularly she liked her art teacher, Miss Dietrich, the tall red-haired woman who taught her law and order in doing things; and the beauty of working step by step until a job is done; a picture finished; a design created; or a block print carved out of nothing but an idea and a smooth square of linoleum, inked, proofs made, and finally put down on paper—clean, sharp, beautiful, individual, unlike any other in the world, thus making the paper have a meaning nobody else could give it except Nancy Lee. That was the wonderful thing about true creation. You made something nobody else on earth could make—but you.

Miss Dietrich was the kind of teacher who brought out the best in her students—but their own best, not anybody else's copied best. For anybody else's best, great though it might be, even Michelangelo's, wasn't enough to please Miss Dietrich dealing with the creative impulses of young men and women living in an American city in the Middle West, and being American.

Nancy Lee was proud of being American, a Negro American with blood out of Africa a long time ago, too many generations back to count. But her parents had taught her the beauties of Africa, its strength, its song, its mighty rivers, its early smelting of iron, its building of the pyramids, and its ancient and important civilizations. And Miss Dietrich had discovered for her the sharp and humorous lines of African sculpture, Benin, Congo, Makonde. Nancy Lee's father was a mail carrier, her mother a social worker in a city settlement house. Both parents had been to Negro colleges in the South. And her mother had gotten a further degree in social work from a Northern university. Her parents were, like most Americans, simple ordinary people who had worked hard and steadily for their education. Now they were trying to make it easier for Nancy Lee to achieve learning than it had been for them. They would be very happy when they heard of the award to their daughter—yet Nancy did not tell them. To surprise them would be better. Besides, there had been a promise.

Casually, one day, Miss Dietrich asked Nancy Lee what color frame she thought would be best on her picture. That had been the first inkling.

"Blue," Nancy Lee said. Although the picture had been entered in the Artist Club contest a month ago, Nancy Lee did not hesitate in her choice of a color for the possible frame since she could still see her picture clearly in her mind's eye—for that picture waiting for the blue frame had come out of her soul, her own life, and had bloomed into miraculous being with Miss Dietrich's help. It was, she knew, the best water color she had painted in her four years as a high-school art student, and she was glad she had made something Miss Dietrich liked well enough to permit her to enter in the contest before she graduated.

It was not a modernistic picture in the sense that you had to look at it a long time to understand what it meant. It was just a simple scene in the city park on a spring day with the trees still leaflessly lacy against the sky, the new grass fresh and green, a flag on a tall pole in the center, children playing, and an old Negro woman sitting on a bench with her head turned. A lot for one picture, to be sure, but it was not there in heavy and final detail like a calendar. Its charm was that everything was light and airy, happy like spring, with a lot of blue sky, paper-white clouds, and air showing through. You could tell that the old Negro woman was looking at the flag, and that the flag was proud in the spring breeze, and that the breeze helped to make the children's dresses billow as they played.

Miss Dietrich had taught Nancy Lee how to paint spring, people, and a breeze on what was only a plain white piece of paper from the supply closet. But Miss

Dietrich had not said make it like any other spring-people-breeze ever seen before. She let it remain Nancy Lee's own. That is how the old Negro woman happened to be there looking at the flag—for in her mind the flag, the spring, and the woman formed a kind of triangle holding a dream Nancy Lee wanted to express. White stars on a blue field, spring, children, ever-growing life, and an old woman. Would the judges at the Artist Club like it?

One wet, rainy April afternoon Miss O'Shay, the girls' vice-principal, sent for Nancy Lee to stop by her office as school closed. Pupils without umbrellas or raincoats were clustered in doorways hoping to make it home between showers. Outside the skies were gray. Nancy Lee's thoughts were suddenly gray, too.

She did not think she had done anything wrong, yet that tight little knot came in her throat just the same as she approached Miss O'Shay's door. Perhaps she had banged her locker too often and too hard. Perhaps the note in French she had written to Sallie halfway across the study hall just for fun had never gotten to Sallie but into Miss O'Shay's hands instead. Or maybe she was failing in some subject and wouldn't be allowed to graduate. Chemistry! A pang went through the pit of her stomach.

She knocked on Miss O'Shay's door. That familiarly solid and competent voice said, "Come in."

Miss O'Shay had a way of making you feel welcome, even if you came to be expelled.

"Sit down, Nancy Lee Johnson," said Miss O'Shay. "I have something to tell you." Nancy Lee sat down. "But I must ask you to promise not to tell anyone yet."

"I won't, Miss O'Shay," Nancy Lee said, wondering what on earth the principal had to say to her.

"You are about to graduate," Miss O'Shay said. "And

we shall miss you. You have been an excellent student, Nancy, and you will not be without honors on the senior list, as I am sure you know."

At that point there was a light knock on the door. Miss O'Shay called out, "Come in," and Miss Dietrich entered. "May I be a part of this, too?" she asked, tall and smiling.

"Of course," Miss O'Shay said. "I was just telling Nancy Lee what we thought of her. But I hadn't gotten around to giving her the news. Perhaps, Miss Dietrich, you'd like to tell her yourself."

Miss Dietrich was always direct. "Nancy Lee," she said, "your picture has won the Artist Club scholarship."

The slender brown girl's eyes widened, her heart jumped, then her throat tightened again. She tried to smile, but instead tears came to her eyes.

"Dear Nancy Lee," Miss O'Shay said, "we are so happy for you." The elderly white woman took her hand and shook it warmly while Miss Dietrich beamed with pride.

Nancy Lee must have danced all the way home. She never remembered quite how she got there through the rain. She hoped she had been dignified. But certainly she hadn't stopped to tell anybody her secret on the way. Raindrops, smiles, and tears mingled on her brown cheeks. She hoped her mother hadn't yet gotten home and that the house was empty. She wanted to have time to calm down and look natural before she had to see anyone. She didn't want to be bursting with excitement—having a secret to contain.

Miss O'Shay's calling her to the office had been in the nature of a preparation and a warning. The kind, elderly vice-principal said she did not believe in catching young ladies unawares, even with honors, so she wished her to know about the coming award. In making acceptance speeches she wanted her to be calm, prepared, not nervous, overcome, and frightened. So Nancy Lee was asked to think what she would say when the scholarship was conferred upon her a few days hence, both at the Friday morning high-school assembly hour when the announcement would be made, and at the evening banquet of the Artist Club. Nancy Lee promised the vice-principal to think calmly about what she would say.

Miss Dietrich had then asked for some facts about her parents, her background, and her life, since such material would probably be desired for the papers. Nancy Lee had told her how, six years before, they had come up from the Deep South, her father having been successful in achieving a transfer from the one post office to another, a thing he had long sought in order to give Nancy Lee a chance to go to school in the North. Now, they lived in a modest Negro neighborhood, went to see the best plays when they came to town, and had been saving to send Nancy Lee to art school, in case she were permitted to enter. But the scholarship would help a great deal, for they were not rich people.

"Now Mother can have a new coat next winter," Nancy Lee thought, "because my tuition will all be covered for the first year. And once in art school, there are other scholarships I can win."

Dreams began to dance through her head, plans and ambitions, beauties she would create for herself, her parents, and the Negro people—for Nancy Lee possessed a deep and reverent race pride. She could see the old woman in her picture (really her grandmother in the South) lifting her head to the bright stars on the flag in the distance. A Negro in America! Often hurt, discriminated against, sometimes lynched—but always there were the stars on the blue body of the flag. Was there any other flag in the world that had so many stars? Nancy Lee thought deeply but she could remember none in all the encyclopedias or geographies she had ever looked into.

"Hitch your wagon to a star," Nancy Lee thought, dancing home in the rain. "Who were our flag-makers?"

Friday morning came, the morning when the world would know—her high-school world, the newspaper world, her mother and dad. Dad could not be there at the assembly to hear the announcement, nor see her prize picture displayed on the stage, nor listen to Nancy Lee's little speech of acceptance, but Mother would be able to come, although Mother was much puzzled as to why Nancy Lee was so insistent she be at school on that particular Friday morning.

When something is happening, something new and fine, something that will change your very life, it is hard to go to sleep at night for thinking about it, and hard to keep your heart from pounding, or a strange little knot of joy from gathering in your throat. Nancy Lee had taken her bath, brushed her hair until it glowed, and had gone to bed thinking about the next day, the big day when, before three thousand students, she would be the one student honored, her painting the one painting to be acclaimed as the best of the year from all the art classes of the city. Her short speech of gratitude was ready. She went over it in her mind, not word for word (because she didn't want it to sound as if she had learned it by heart) but she let the thoughts flow simply and sincerely through her consciousness many times.

When the president of the Artist Club presented her with the medal and scroll of the scholarship award, she would say:

"Judges and members of the Artist Club. I want to

thank you for this award that means so much to me per-
sonally and through me to my people, the colored people
of this city who, sometimes, are discouraged and bewil-
dered, thinking that color and poverty are against them. I
accept this award with gratitude and pride, not for myself
alone, but for my race that believes in American opportunity and American fairness—and the bright stars in our
flag. I thank Miss Dietrich and the teachers who made it
possible for me to have the knowledge and training that
lie behind this honor you have conferred upon my painting. When I came here from the South a few years ago, I
was not sure how you would receive me. You received me
well. You have given me a chance and helped me along
the road I wanted to follow. I suppose the judges know
that every week here at assembly the students of this school
pledge allegiance to the flag. I shall try to be worthy of
that pledge, and of the help and friendship and under-
standing of my fellow citizens of whatever race or creed,
and of our American dream of 'Liberty and justice for
all!' "

That would be her response before the students in the
morning. How proud and happy the Negro pupils would
be, perhaps almost as proud as they were of the one colored star on the football team. Her mother would probably cry with happiness. Thus Nancy Lee went to sleep
dreaming of a wonderful tomorrow.

The bright sunlight of an April morning woke her.
There was breakfast with her parents—their half-amused
and puzzled faces across the table, wondering what could
be this secret that made her eyes so bright. The swift walk
to school; the clock in the tower almost nine; hundreds of
pupils streaming into the long, rambling old building that
was the city's largest high school; the sudden quiet of the

homeroom after the bell rang; then the teacher opening her record book to call the roll. But just before she began, she looked across the room until her eyes located Nancy Lee.

"Nancy," she said, "Miss O'Shay would like to see you in her office, please."

Nancy Lee rose and went out while the names were being called and the word *present* added its period to each name. Perhaps, Nancy Lee thought, the reporters from the papers had already come. Maybe they wanted to take her picture before assembly, which wasn't until ten o'clock. (Last year they had had the photograph of the winner of the award in the morning papers as soon as the announcement had been made.)

Nancy Lee knocked at Miss O'Shay's door.

"Come in."

The vice-principal stood at her desk. There was no one else in the room. It was very quiet.

"Sit down, Nancy Lee," she said. Miss O'Shay did not smile. There was a long pause. The seconds went by slowly. "I do not know how to tell you what I have to say," the elderly woman began, her eyes on the papers on her desk. "I am indignant and ashamed for myself and for this city." Then she lifted her eyes and looked at Nancy Lee in the neat blue dress sitting there before her. "You are not to receive the scholarship this morning."

Outside in the hall the electric bells announcing the first period rang, loud and interminably long. Miss O'Shay remained silent. To the brown girl there in the chair, the room grew suddenly smaller, smaller, smaller, and there was no air. She could not speak.

Miss O'Shay said, "When the committee learned that you were colored, they changed their plans."

Still Nancy Lee said nothing, for there was no air to give breath to her lungs.

"Here is the letter from the committee, Nancy Lee." Miss O'Shay picked it up and read the final paragraph to her.

" 'It seems to us wiser to arbitrarily rotate the award among the various high schools of the city from now on. And especially in this case since the student chosen happens to be colored, a circumstance which unfortunately, had we known, might have prevented this embarrassment. But there have never been any Negro students in the local art school, and the presence of one there might create difficulties for all concerned. We have high regard for the quality of Nancy Lee Johnson's talent, but we do not feel it would be fair to honor it with the Artist Club award.' " Miss O'Shay paused. She put the letter down.

"Nancy Lee, I am very sorry to have to give you this message."

"But my speech," Nancy Lee said, "was about . . . ." The words stuck in her throat. " . . . about America. . . ."

Miss O'Shay had risen, she turned her back and stood looking out the window at the spring tulips in the school yard.

"I thought, since the award would be made at assembly right after our oath of allegiance," the words tumbled almost hysterically from Nancy Lee's throat now, "I would put part of the flag salute in my speech. You know, Miss O'Shay, that part about 'liberty and justice for all.' "

"I know," said Miss O'Shay slowly facing the room again. "But America is only what we who believe in it, make it. I am Irish. You may not know, Nancy Lee, but years ago we were called the dirty Irish, and mobs rioted against us in the big cities, and we were invited to go back where we came from. But we didn't go. And we didn't give up, because we believed in the American dream, and in our power to make that dream come true. Difficulties, yes. Mountains to climb, yes. Discouragements to face, yes. Democracy to make, yes. That is it, Nancy Lee! We still have in this world of ours democracy to *make*. You and I, Nancy Lee. But the premise and the base are here, the lines of the Declaration of Independence and the words of Lincoln are here, and the stars in our flag. Those who deny you this scholarship do not know the meaning of those stars, but it's up to us to make them know. As a teacher in the public schools of this city, I myself will go before the school board and ask them to remove from our system the offer of any prizes or awards denied to any student because of race or color."

Suddenly Miss O'Shay stopped speaking. Her clear, clear blue eyes looked into those of the girl before her. The woman's eyes were full of strength and courage. "Lift up your head, Nancy Lee, and smile at me."

Miss O'Shay stood against the open window with the green lawn and the tulips beyond, the sunlight tangled in her gray hair, her voice an electric flow of strength to the hurt spirit of Nancy Lee. The Abolitionists who believed in freedom when there was slavery must have been like that. The first white teachers who went into the Deep South to teach the freed slaves must have been like that. All those who stand against ignorance, narrowness, hate, and mud on stars must be like that.

Nancy Lee lifted her head and smiled. The bell for assembly rang. She went through the long hall filled with students toward the auditorium.

"There will be other awards," Nancy Lee thought. "There're schools in other cities. This won't keep me down. But when I'm a woman, I'll fight to see that these things don't happen to other girls as this has happened to me. And men and women like Miss O'Shay will help me."

She took her seat among the seniors. The doors of the auditorium closed. As the principal came onto the platform, the students rose and turned their eyes to the flag on the stage.

One hand went to the heart, the other outstretched toward the flag. Three thousand voices spoke. Among them was the voice of a dark girl whose cheeks were suddenly wet with tears, " . . . one nation indivisible, with liberty and justice for all."

"That is the land we must make," she thought.

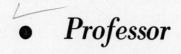 **Professor**

● *PROMPTLY* at seven a big car drew up in front of the Booker T. Washington Hotel, and a white chauffeur in uniform got out and went toward the door,

97

intending to ask at the desk for a colored professor named T. Walton Brown. But the professor was already sitting in the lobby, a white scarf around his neck and his black overcoat ready to button over his dinner clothes.

As soon as the chauffeur entered, the professor approached. "Mr. Chandler's car?" he asked hesitantly.

"Yes, sir," said the white chauffeur to the neat little Negro. "Are you Dr. Walton Brown?"

"I am," said the professor, smiling and bowing a little.

The chauffeur opened the street door for Dr. Brown, then ran to the car and held the door open there, too. Inside the big car and on the long black running board as well, the lights came on. The professor stepped in among the soft cushions, the deep rug, and the cut glass vases holding flowers. With the greatest of deference the chauffeur quickly tucked a covering of fur about the professor's knees, closed the door, entered his own seat in front beyond the glass partition, and the big car purred away. Within the lobby of the cheap hotel a few ill-clad Negroes watched the whole procedure in amazement.

"A big shot!" somebody said.

At the corner as the car passed, two or three ash-colored children ran across the street in front of the wheel, their skinny legs and poor clothes plain in the glare of the headlights as the chauffeur slowed down to let them pass. Then the car turned and ran the whole length of a Negro street that was lined with pawn shops, beer joints, pig's knuckle stands, cheap movies, hairdressing parlors, and other ramshackle places of business patronized by the poor blacks of the district. Inside the big car the professor, Dr. Walton Brown, regretted that in all the large Midwestern cities where he had lectured on his present tour in behalf of his college, the main Negro streets presented the same sleazy and disagreeable appearance: pig's knuckle joints, pawn shops, beer parlors—and houses of vice, no doubt—save that these latter, at least, did not hang out their signs.

The professor looked away from the unpleasant sight of this typical Negro street, poor and unkempt. He looked ahead through the glass at the dignified white neck of the uniformed chauffeur in front of him. The professor in his dinner clothes, his brown face even browner above the white silk scarf at his neck, felt warm and comfortable under the fur rug. But he felt, too, a little unsafe at being driven through the streets of this city on the edge of the South in an expensive car, by a white chauffeur.

"But, then," he thought, "this is the wealthy Mr. Ralph P. Chandler's car, and surely no harm can come to me here. The Chandlers are a power in the Middle West, and in the South as well. Theirs is one of the great fortunes of America. In philanthropy, nobody exceeds them in well-planned generosity on a large and highly publicized scale. They are a power in Negro education, too. That is why I am visiting them tonight at their invitation."

Just now the Chandlers were interested in the little Negro college at which the professor taught. They wanted to make it one of the major Negro colleges of America. And in particular the Chandlers were interested in his Department of Sociology. They were thinking of endowing a chair of research there and employing a man of ability for it. A Ph.D. and a scholar. A man of some prestige, like the professor. For his *The Sociology of Prejudice* (that restrained and conservative study of Dr. T. Walton Brown's) had recently come to the attention of the Chandler Committee. And a representative of their philanthropies, visiting the campus, had conversed with the professor at some length about his book and his views. This representative of the Committee found Dr. Brown highly gratifying, because in almost every case the professor's views agreed with the white man's own.

"A fine, sane, dependable young Negro," was the description that came to the Chandler Committee from their traveling representative.

So now the power himself, Mr. Ralph P. Chandler, and Mrs. Chandler, learning that he was lecturing at one of the colored churches of the town, had invited him to dinner at their mansion in this city on the edge of the South. Their car had come to call for him at the colored Booker T. Washington Hotel—where the hot water was always cold, the dresser drawers stuck, and the professor shivered as he got into his dinner clothes; and the bellboys, anxious for a tip, had asked him twice that evening if he needed a half pint or a woman.

But now he was in this big warm car and they were moving swiftly down a fine boulevard, the black slums far behind them. The professor was glad. He had been very much distressed at having the white chauffeur call for him at this cheap hotel in what really amounted to the red-light district of the town. But, then, none of the white hotels in this American city would house Negroes, no matter how cultured they might be. Marian Anderson herself had been unable to find decent accommodations there, so the colored papers said, on the day of her concert.

Sighing, the professor looked out of the car at the wide lawns and fine homes that lined the beautiful well-lighted boulevard where white people lived. After a time the car turned into a fashionable suburban road and he saw no more houses, but only ivy-hung walls, neat shrubs, and boxwoods that indicated not merely homes beyond but vast estates. Shortly the car whirled into a paved driveway, past a small lodge, through a park full of fountains and trees, and up to a private house as large as a hotel. From a tall portico a great hanging lantern cast a soft glow on the black and chrome body of the big car. The white chauffeur jumped out and deferentially opened the door for the colored professor. An English butler welcomed him at the entrance and took his coat, hat, and scarf. Then he led the professor into a large drawing room where two men and a woman were standing chatting near the fireplace.

The professor hesitated, not knowing who was who; but Mr. and Mrs. Chandler came forward, introduced themselves, shook hands, and in turn presented their other guest of the evening, Dr. Bulwick of the local Municipal College—a college that Dr. Brown recalled did *not* admit Negroes.

"I am happy to know you," said Dr. Bulwick. "I am also a sociologist."

"I have heard of you," said Dr. Brown graciously.

The butler came with sherry in a silver pitcher. They sat down, and the whites began to talk politely, to ask Dr. Brown about his lecture tour, if his audiences were good, if they were mostly Negro or mixed, and if there was much interest in his college, much money being given.

Then Dr. Bulwick began to ask about his book, *The Sociology of Prejudice*, where he got his material, under whom he had studied, and if he thought the Negro Problem would ever be solved.

Dr. Brown said genially, "We are making progress," which was what he always said, though he often felt he was lying.

"Yes," said Dr. Bulwick, "that is very true. Why, at our city college here we've been conducting some fine inter-racial experiments. I have had several colored ministers and high-school teachers visit my classes. We found them most intelligent people."

In spite of himself Dr. Brown had to say, "But you have no colored students at your college, have you?"

"No," said Dr. Bulwick, "and that is too bad! But that is one of our difficulties here. There is no Municipal College for Negroes—although nearly forty per cent of our population is colored. Some of us have thought it might be wise to establish a separate junior college for our Negroes, but the politicians opposed it on the score of no funds. And we cannot take them as students on our campus. That, at present, is impossible. It's too bad."

"But do you not think, Dr. Brown," interposed Mrs. Chandler, who wore diamonds on her wrists and smiled every time she spoke, "do you not think *your* people are happier in schools of their own—that it is really better for both groups not to mix them?"

In spite of himself Dr. Brown replied, "That depends, Mrs. Chandler. I could not have gotten my degree in any schools of our own."

"True, true," said Mr. Chandler. "Advanced studies, of course, cannot be gotten. But when your colleges are developed—as we hope they will be, and our Committee plans to aid in their development—when their departments are headed by men like yourself, for instance, then you can no longer say, 'That depends.'"

"You are right," Dr. Brown agreed diplomatically, coming to himself and thinking of his mission in that house. "You are right," Dr. Brown said, thinking too of that endowed chair of sociology and himself in the chair, the six thousand dollars a year that he would probably be paid, the surveys he might make and the books he could publish. "You are right," said Dr. Brown diplomatically to Ralph

P. Chandler. But in the back of his head was that ghetto street full of sleazy misery he had just driven through, and the segregated hotel where the hot water was always cold, and the colored churches where he lectured, and the Jim Crow schools where Negroes always had less equipment and far less money than white institutions; and that separate justice of the South where his people sat on trial but the whites were judge and jury forever; and all the segregated Jim Crow things that America gave Negroes and that were never equal to the things she gave the whites. But Dr. Brown said, "You are right, Mr. Chandler," for, after all, Mr. Chandler had the money!

So he began to talk earnestly to the Chandlers there in the warm drawing room about the need for bigger and better black colleges, for more and more surveys of *Negro* life, and a well-developed department of sociology at his own little institution.

"Dinner is served," said the butler.

They rose and went into a dining room where there were flowers on the table and candles, white linen and silver, and where Dr. Brown was seated at the right of the hostess and the talk was light over the soup, but serious and sociological again by the time the meat was served.

"The American Negro must not be taken in by communism," Dr. Bulwick was saying with great positiveness as the butler passed the peas.

"He won't," agreed Dr. Brown. "I assure you, our leadership stands squarely against it." He looked at the Chandlers and bowed. "All the best people stand against it."

"America has done too much for the Negro," said Mr. Chandler, "for him to seek to destroy it."

Dr. Brown bobbed and bowed.

"In your *Sociology of Prejudice*," said Dr. Bulwick, "I

highly approve of the closing note, your magnificent appeal to the old standards of Christian morality and the simple concepts of justice by which America functions."

"Yes," said Dr. Brown, nodding his dark head and thinking suddenly how on six thousand dollars a year he might take his family to South America in the summer where for three months they wouldn't feel like Negroes. "Yes, Dr. Bulwick," he nodded, "I firmly believe as you do that if the best elements of both races came together in Christian fellowship, we would solve this problem of ours."

"How beautiful," said Mrs. Chandler.

"And practical, too," said her husband. "But now to come back to your college—university, I believe you call it—to bring that institution up to really first-class standards you would need . . . ?"

"We would need . . ." said Dr. Brown, speaking as a mouthpiece of the administration, and speaking, too, as mouthpiece for the Negro students of his section of the South, and speaking for himself as a once ragged youth who had attended the college when its rating was lower than that of a Northern high school so that he had to study two years in Boston before he could enter a white college, when he had worked nights as redcap in the station and then as a waiter for seven years until he got his Ph.D., and then couldn't get a job in the North but had to go back down South to the work where he was now—but which might develop into a glorious opportunity at six thousand dollars a year to make surveys and put down figures that other scholars might study to get their Ph.D.'s, and that would bring him in enough to just once take his family on a vacation to South America where they wouldn't feel that they were Negroes. "We would need, Mr. Chandler, . . ."

And the things Dr. Brown's little college needed were small enough in the eyes of the Chandlers. The sane and conservative way in which Dr. Brown presented his case delighted the philanthropic heart of the Chandlers. And Mr. Chandler and Dr. Bulwick both felt that instead of building a junior college for Negroes in their own town they could rightfully advise local colored students to go down South to that fine little campus where they had a professor of their own race like Dr. Brown.

Over the coffee, in the drawing room, they talked about the coming theatrical season. And Mrs. Chandler spoke of how she loved Negro singers, and smiled and smiled.

In due time the professor rose to go. The car was called and he shook hands with Dr. Bulwick and the Chandlers. The white people were delighted with Dr. Brown. He could see it in their faces, just as in the past he could always tell as a waiter when he had pleased a table full of whites by tender steaks and good service.

"Tell the president of your college he shall hear from us shortly," said the Chandlers. "We'll probably send a man down again soon to talk to him about his expansion program." And they bowed farewell.

As the car sped him back toward town, Dr. Brown sat under its soft fur rug among the deep cushions and thought how with six thousand dollars a year earned by dancing properly to the tune of Jim Crow education, he could carry his whole family to South America for a summer where they wouldn't need to feel like Negroes.

● *Name in the*
Papers

● *I ALWAYS* did wonder what I'd do if some husband or other came home some time and caught me with his wife. Now it's happened. I'm reading about it in the papers.

Her name was Deedee, but that was the only thing French about her. Otherwise she was pure Harlem.

I met her at a party and the drinks were mixed. How should I know she was married? She came in alone, so I took her under my wing. There were too many other wolves around to leave her unprotected.

I said, "Have one."

She said, "Sure."

The next time they turned on the radio we got together and danced the rest of the evening. She was 100%! I liked her style, so I said, "Baby, who's the big boss?"

She said, "He works nights."

I said, "That's the old gag, honey. So do I."

She said, "Aw, now, you quit!"

I said, "I'm not made that way."

By that time she was tickled all over. Me, too.

I said, "Have one more."

She said, "Sure."

I mixed it myself. Then some guy sat down at the piano and started playing that old song about the Lazy River and the old mill stream.

I said, "I can't stand it no more. Let's go."

Of all the homes to stay away from, I'm tellin' you now, avoid those where the husband works nights. I could tell she was really married the minute I got in her door. The house had a no-place-like-home look.

I said, "Honey, are you *sure* he works all night?"

She said, "Of course, he does. I wouldn't lie to you."

But somehow, neither one of us realized night was nearly up then! We'd left that party pretty late. (And I had really *mixed* those drinks!) Besides, you know how long it stays dark on winter mornings!

It was dark that day, I tell you! Because the next thing

I knew, her husband was home. He came right home at daybreak like a good husband. The afternoon papers said he arrived at seven A.M., but it seemed like the middle of the night to me. Nevertheless, he arrived. When I saw him, I said, "Hy, Buddy!"

He said, "Hy, hell!" And pulled out a pistol.

Now, that was the moment I had always wondered about. Just what would I do? Fight, run, or holler? But the truth is, I didn't do anything—because the next thing I knew I was in the hospital, shot everywhere but in my big toe. He fired on me point-blank—and barefooted. I was nothing but a target.

"Nurse, is there anything about me in the *Daily News*? Is my name in the papers?"

Powder-White Faces

● *IT WAS* good to feel the sea spray on his face again, to look up at the stars rocking in the sky, to breathe the great, clean rush of wind from the open ocean as the deck swayed beneath his feet.

111

The little old freighter had slipped down the East River past the lights of New York like a glittering wall to starboard. Charlie Lee, messboy, lit a cigarette, inhaled once, and threw it into the water.

"We're off, heh, mate?" said a white seaman leaning on the rail beside the Oriental.

"Yep," Charlie Lee said. "Long gone this time."

The Statue of Liberty holding its light moved back into the darkness. Staten Island sliding by, Brooklyn on the other side starry with lights, moved back into darkness.

"Goodnight," said the seaman, "I'm turnin' in."

" 'Night," said Charlie Lee. He lit another cigarette, and listened to the heavy beat of the engines settle into an even rhythm of full steam ahead, a beat that would not be silent for several weeks to come. In a certain steady way the waves hit the boatside, the masts rocked against the sky, the weight of the rail pressed on Charlie's chest and then fell away. All this sea movement would go on for many days. Charlie was glad his next port would be Cape Town, thousands of miles from Manhattan—for that morning Charlie had killed a woman.

As Charlie Lee stood by the ship's side looking out into the watery darkness of the Atlantic, he tried to think why he had done it. But he could not think why, he could only *feel* why. He could feel again, standing by the rail, all the hatred and anger of a lifetime that had suddenly that morning collected in his heart and gathered in his fingers at the sight of a white face and a red mouth on the pillow beneath him.

Charlie Lee had killed a *white* woman just twelve hours ago.

Charlie Lee. That wasn't his real name. Charlie had

almost forgotten his real name. But Charlie Lee was a good name, he thought. It didn't sound oriental like the names of most of the people on the little American possession in the Pacific from which he had come. It was better than a name like Ah Woo or Kakawali or Chung Sing.

But the name didn't really matter. What mattered was that Charlie's face was brown, his eyes slanted, and his hair heavy and black like a Chinese. Because of his color and perhaps his eyes, American ships wouldn't hire him for any work but a steward's or a kitchen boy's. American or English officers on his own island wouldn't give him a clerk's job if they could find a white person to fill it. And no white woman would marry him unless she were down and out.

But a white man, very long ago, had taken his youngest sister for a mistress, and she had borne him four children.

That was before Charlie grew up, changed his name, and went away to sea as a cabin boy on a tramp steamer bound for Frisco. For nearly ten years Charlie had never been back home. Sailing all the world. The Pacific, the Atlantic, the Mediterranean. Many cities, many people. White, brown, and yellow people. Stopping a while to work ashore in California vineyards; one winter as a Santa Barbara houseboy: another winter in a New York elevator on Riverside Drive, up and down, up and down. And between times, the sea, the great, clean, old sea rocking beneath his feet—like tonight.

Now, Charlie Lee stood at the tramp's rail with the wind blowing in his face wondering why he had killed that white woman this morning. He had never killed anybody in his life before. And this woman had really done nothing to him. Not *this* woman. Then why did he kill *her*? But when he tried to figure it out, he kept remembering other white women (not the one he had killed, but *other* women), port-town women, taxi-dance-hall women, women with powder-white faces who took all they could get from him and then let him go, called him names, kicked him out, or had him beaten up.

It began with the girls in Mollie's Tropical Beer Garden where he had worked at home out in the Pacific before he grew up and changed his name. There he ran errands for the white hostesses and the American marines. There, he often heard the girls declare they couldn't have anything to do with a native because if they did Uncle Sam's boys wouldn't have anything to do with them. So the policy of Mollie's Beer Garden was WHITE ONLY insofar as her customers went. (There was a sign over the bar to that effect.) And although the waiters were native brown boys, the bartender—the only one who got a salary—was Irish. The brown boys worked for tips alone.

When Charlie went away to sea, the next foreign women he knew were White Russians under the carnival lights of Shanghai, rapacious females, hungry and diseased, who haunted the bars, dives, and dance halls, sleeping with anyone who could pay them, and picking pockets in the bargain. They cleaned Charlie out of all his money while his ship was in dock. And the doctors put him in the Marine Hospital when he reached San Francisco ill.

When he got better, he found a job in the grape orchards on the coast and experienced all the prejudices of white California toward the brown people from across the Pacific. Even if you were from an *American* island, it didn't seem to make any difference.

After two years in California Charlie went to sea again as a cabin boy on a freighter. San Diego, Colon, Havana, the Gulf ports. Then he got in jail, for the first time, at New Orleans.

All the messboys went out together their first night in port, to a wineshop on St. Louis Street. Along the street the shutters kept clicking and white women kept looking out at the little Orientals in their broad-shouldered suits and highly polished shoes. Sometimes the women whispered, "Come in, baby." But the boys kept on to a place where they were sure they were welcome, for in this wineshop there were women, too. Rather faded women, it's true, a little old or a little ugly or a little droopy—but the best the Italian proprietor could get for a bar that catered to yellow-brown boys from the ships, for seldom did white sailors come there, and almost never men of the city.

But tonight, by chance, a group of white men did come —not sailors, but young Southern rowdies about town looking for fun. They were already half drunk, and they weren't used to seeing (as sailors would have been) brown men and white women mixing. They felt hurt about it as they stood drinking at the bar. They felt insulted. They got mad. They wanted to protect white womanhood.

"Let's clean out the spicks," one of them whispered.

A big guy turned on Charlie.

"Take your eyes off that white woman, coon," he said, hitting him across the mouth, wham! without warning.

Charlie staggered to his feet. His friends drew knives. The girls screamed and gathered behind the white men. Fists flew. A fight was on.

The next thing Charlie knew, he regained consciousness in a cell. Alone, his face battered, his clothes torn, his money and watch gone, he felt sick and his head whirled. There were iron bars all around him like a cage. His body hurt. And his soul hurt, too.

The last thing he remembered before the big white fellow knocked him out was that the girl whom he had just treated to a drink suddenly spat in his face. Charlie never forgot that. The judge gave him ten days in jail for disturbing the peace, and he missed his boat. For nearly a month he went hungry in New Orleans, but finally he managed to ship out on a coastwise steamer to New York. The salt of the sea healed the purple bruises on his face.

In Manhattan he got a job as elevator boy in a busy house on the Drive. Nights he spent in the taxi-dance halls above Columbus Circle frequented by sleek-haired little brown fellows, Filipinos, Hawaiians, and Chinese, dancing and dancing to rhumbas that were like the palm trees swaying in his native islands.

There were lots of white girls, powdered pink and blonde, who worked in these dance halls and lived on the boys who went to dance there. Once Charlie was in love with one of these hostesses. He kept bringing her all his money every week, until she said one night, "Darling, you don't make enough for me. Why don't you gamble or something and get some real dough?"

So Charlie began to lose all his wages trying to win more for her. Every week he lost. He worried about her, kept stopping the elevator at the wrong floors with her on his mind, and finally got fired from his job. Of course she left him.

When he found work again it was as houseboy for a rich young man named Richards who had an apartment on lower Fifth Avenue.

He had plenty to do, but he was well paid. He liked the boss, and the boss liked him. But Charlie didn't like Mr. Richards' mistress. He found her too much like the girls in the taxi-dance halls, or in St. Louis Street in New Orleans, hard, rapacious, and crude. But sometimes, for days, he wouldn't see Mr. Richards—only this woman. And, as time went on, she became more and more familiar with Charlie, said things to him that she shouldn't say to a servant, kidded him, walked around before him in pink silk things that were only shadows, smiling. Charlie hated her. Even when she put all her jewels on—blonde as a beauty shop and sprinkled with perfume—she still made him think of Shanghai and the hungry little Russian girls of Avenue Joffre who had stolen his money and left him ill years ago, and the white woman who spat in his face in New Orleans, and the dance-hall girl who left him when he went broke and had no job.

"Why can't Mr. Richards see what she's like?" Charlie wondered. "Me see."

Yet she was always nice to Charlie. Bold and invitingly nice. Even when she asked him to go out and buy dope for her and he refused, she didn't really mind. She only purred, "Don't tell Richie, will you?" as she went to the phone to order the white powder from a druggist she knew.

Now, Charlie recalled as he stood by the ship's rail, she and Mr. Richards kept talking about the dog races last night at the table during dinner. Later they went out and returned long after midnight. Charlie didn't hear them come in, but early in the morning the telephone rang. Long distance, Chicago calling. He woke Mr. Richards, who got all excited as he listened to the voice at the other end of the line. He kept talking about a merger, merger, merger. Finally he said, "I'll be there today." Then he called Charlie to pack his bag. "Flying to Chicago right away," he said. "Call a cab."

He kissed his blonde woman lying drowsy on the silken bed and, without eating, rushed out at dawn. Charlie didn't see him any more. In a few minutes the tragedy happened.

The blonde woman said, "Come here, Charlie." When Charlie came near the bed, she took him by his silky hair and pulled him down close to her breast.

"You're a cute China boy!" she said. "Kiss me."

But Charlie drew away. A sudden combination of anger and loathing came into his eyes. Fear and hatred. Distrust, suspicion, contempt for her lack of loyalty. What do you want with me? What's your game? What are you trying to gyp me out of? What do you want to do? I'm not your color! I know you too well—you and all your kind! You never played square by me, just like you don't play square by Mr. Richards. You white women, you cheats!

"Charlie," she said.

His brown hands gently sought her face, her chin. And suddenly closed on her throat. She did not even scream. Her mouth opened, but was silent. No breath, no sound. And Charlie didn't know why he did it.

Charlie suddenly remembered three Americans who killed a brown man in Honolulu over a white woman. He remembered the iron bars around him in New Orleans. And the powder-white faces of the Russian girls in Shanghai. And the hostesses in Mollie's Beer Garden, FOR WHITE ONLY. All the hidden resentment of years seemed to collect in his heart and gather in his fingers as the red mouth slowly opened on the pillow beneath him.

He did not want her. He only wanted to kill her—this woman who became suddenly *all* white women to him.

As he locked the apartment and went out into the early morning air he smelled the sea again—the sea into which you can pour all the filth of the world, but the water never gets dirty.

Rouge High

TWO streetwalkers came in and began to powder their faces. The waiter slid a couple of glasses of water along the counter and was about to take their order when a tall young fellow entered and knocked one of the girls plumb off the stool with a blow in the face.

"Here, honey! Take it! Here it is!" she began to yell.

Before she got up off the floor, she took a wrinkled bill from somewhere down in her bosom and gave it to him.

"Tryin' to hold out on me," said the fellow as he turned on his heel and left.

The girl got back up on the stool and went on powdering her face. She didn't shed a single tear.

"Ham and eggs, scrambled," said her companion.

"Nothin' but coffee for me," said the one who had been hit. "Them shots the doc gave me this mornin' made me sick. I can't eat a thing."

"Shots are hell," said the other one. "But, say, girlie, listen. What made Bunny think you was holdin' out on him?"

"He didn't think it, he knew it! He's pretty smart at figgerin' out what a John'll pay—that's why he's always on the corner lookin' 'em over when they come along. Bunny's an old hand at gettin' his."

"Then why didn't you give it to him then?"

"Aw, he ain't so wise as he thinks he is," said the girl as the waiter put her cup of coffee down in front of her. "Listen, I stole that last customer's pocketbook, too. And, believe me, I ain't splittin' these extra bucks with nobody!"

From somewhere under her clothes she pulled out a man's brown wallet, took out the money, and tossed the pocketbook across the counter to the waiter.

"Hey, kid," she said, "put that way down in the garbage can, underneath the coffee grounds. Get me?"

"I got you," the waiter said.

"What you gonna do, buy a new dress?" asked the other girl enviously.

"Naw, I got to pay the doctor for them shots."

She drank her coffee. When they went out, she gave the waiter a good tip.

"Honey," said the other girl as she opened the door, "your eye's gettin' black where Bunny hit you. Put a little more powder on it—or else rouge high."

● *On the Way Home*

● CARL was not what you would call a drinking man. Not that he had any moral scruples about drinking, for he prided himself on being broad-minded. But he had always been told that his father (whom he couldn't remember) was a drunkard. So in the back of his head, he didn't really feel it right to get drunk. Except for perhaps a glass of wine on holidays, or a bottle of beer if he was out with a party and didn't want to be conspicuous, he was a teetotaler.

Carl had promised his mother not to drink *at all*. He was an only child, fond of his mother. But she had raised him with almost too much kindness. To adjust himself to people who were less kind had been hard. But since there were no good jobs in Sommerville, he came away to Chicago to work. Every month, for a Sunday, he went back home, taking the four o'clock bus Saturday afternoon, which put him off in front of his boyhood door in time for supper—with country butter, fresh milk, and home-made bread.

After supper he would go uptown with his mother in the cool of evening, if it was summer, to do her Saturday-night shopping. Or if it was winter, they might go over to a neighbor's house and pop corn or drink cider. Or friends might come to their home and sit around the parlor talking and playing old records on an old victrola—Sousa's marches, Nora Bayes, Bert Williams, Caruso—records that most other people had long ago thrown away or forgotten. It was fun, old-fashioned, and very different from the rum parties most of his office friends indulged in in Chicago.

Carl had definitely promised his mother and himself not to drink. But this particular afternoon, he stood in front of a long counter in a liquor store on Clark Street and heard himself say, strangely enough, "A bottle of wine."

"What kind of wine?" the clerk asked brusquely.

"That kind," Carl answered, pointing to a row of tall yellow bottles on the middle shelf. It just happened that his finger stopped at the yellow bottles. He did not know the names or brands of wines.

"That's sweet wine," the clerk said.

"That's all right," Carl affirmed, for he wanted to get the wine quickly and go.

The clerk wrapped the bottle, made change, and turned to another customer. Carl took the bottle and went out. He walked slowly, yet he could hardly wait to get to his room. He had never been so anxious to drink before. He might have stopped at a bar, since he passed many, but he was not used to drinking at bars. So he went to his room.

It was quiet in the big, dark, old rooming house. There was no one in the hall as he went up the wide, creaking staircase. All the roomers were at work. It was Tuesday. He would have been at work, too, had he not received at the office about noon a wire that his mother was suddenly very ill, and he had better come home. He knew there was no bus until four o'clock. It was one now. He would get ready to go soon. But he needed a drink. Did not men sometimes drink to steady their nerves? In novels they took a swig of brandy—but brandy made Carl sick. Wine would be better—milder.

In his room he tore open the package and uncorked the bottle even before he hung his hat in the closet. He took his toothbrush out of a glass on his dresser and poured the glass a third full of the amber-yellow wine. He tried to keep himself from wondering if his mother was going to die.

"Please, no!" he prayed. He drank the wine.

He sat down on the bed to get his breath back. That climb up the steps had never taken his breath before, but now his heart was beating fast, and sweat had come out on his brow, so he took off his coat, tie, shirt, and got ready to wash his face.

He had better pack his bag first. Then, he suddenly thought, he had no present for his mother—but he caught himself in the middle of the thought. This was not Saturday, not one of his monthly Saturdays when he went home. This was Tuesday and there was this telegram from the Rossiters in his pocket that had suddenly broken the whole rhythm of his life:

YOUR MOTHER GRAVELY ILL STOP COME HOME AT ONCE.

John and Nellie Rossiter had been neighbors since childhood. They would not frighten him needlessly. His mother must be very ill indeed, so he need not think of taking her a present. He went to the closet door to pull out the suitcase, but his hands did not move. The wine, amber-yellow in its tall bottle, stood on the dresser beside him. Warm, sweet, forbidden.

There was no one in the room. Nobody in the whole house perhaps except the landlady. Nobody really in all Chicago to talk to in his trouble. With a mother to take care of on a small salary, room rent, a class at business college, books to buy, there's not much time left to make friends or take girls out. In a big city it's hard for a strange young man to know people.

Carl poured the glass full of wine again—drank it. Then he opened the top drawer, took out his toilet articles and put them on the bed. From the second drawer he took a couple of shirts. Maybe three would be better, or four. This was not a week end. Perhaps he had better take some extra clothing—in case his mother was ill long, and he had to stay a week or more. Perhaps he'd better take his dark suit in case she . . .

It hit him in the stomach like a fist. A pang of fear spread over his whole body. He sat down trembling on the bed.

"Buck up, old man!" The sound of his own voice comforted him. He smiled weakly at his face in the mirror. "Be a man!"

He filled the glass full this time and drank it without stopping. He had never drunk so much wine before and this was warm, sweet, and palatable. He stood, threw his shoulders back, and felt suddenly tall as though his head were touching the ceiling. Then, for no reason at all, he looked at himself in the mirror and began to sing. He made up a song out of nowhere that repeated itself over and over:

> *In the spring the roses*
> *In the spring begin to sing*
> *Roses in the spring*
> *Begin to sing . . .*

He took off his clothes, put on his bathrobe, carefully drained the bottle, then went down the hall to the bathroom, still singing. He ran a tub full of water, climbed in, and sat down. The water in the tub was warm like the wine. He felt good remembering a dark grassy slope in a corner of his mother's yard where he played with a little girl when he was very young at home. His mother came out, separated them, and sent the little girl away because she wasn't of a decent family. But now his mother would never dismiss another little girl be—

Carl sat up quickly in the tub, splashed water over his back and over his head. Drunk? What's the matter? What's the matter with you? Thinking of your mother that way and maybe she's dy— Say! Listen, don't you know you have to catch a four o'clock bus? And here he was getting drunk before he even started on the way home. He trembled. His heart beat fast, so fast that he lay down in the tub to catch his breath, all but his head covered with the warm water.

To lie quiet that way was fine. Still and quiet. Tuesday. Everybody working at the office. And here he was, Carl Anderson, lying quiet in a deep tub of warm water. Maybe someday in a few years with a little money saved up, and no expenses at home, and a car to take girls out in the spring,

> *When the roses sing*
> *In the spring . . .*

He had a good voice and the song that he had made up himself about roses sounded good with wine on his breath as he sang, so he stood up in the tub, grabbed a towel, and began to sing quite lustily. Suddenly there was a knock at the door.

"What's going on in there?"

It was the landlady's voice in the hall outside. She must have heard him singing downstairs.

"Nothing, Mrs. Dyer! Nothing! I just feel like singing."

"Mr. Anderson? Is that you? What're you doing in the house this time of day?"

"I'm on the way home to see my mother. She . . ."

"You sound happier than a lark about it. I couldn't imagine . . ."

He heard the landlady's feet shuffling off down the stairs, back to her ironing.

"She's . . ." His head began to go round and round. "My mother's . . ." His eyes suddenly burned. To step out of the tub, he held tightly to the sides. Drunk, that's what he was! Drunk!

He lurched down the hall, fell across the bed in his room, and buried his head in the pillows. He stretched his arms above his head to the rods of the bedstand. He felt ashamed. With his head in the pillows all was dark. His mother dying? No! No! But he was drunk.

In the dark he seemed to feel his mother's hand on his head when he was a little boy, and her voice saying, "Be sweet, Carl. Be a good boy. Keep clean. Mother loves you. She'll look out for you. Be sweet—and remember what you're taught at home."

Then the roses in the song he had made up and the wine he had drunk began to go around and around in his head and he felt as if he had betrayed his mother and home singing about roses and spring and dreaming of cars and pretty girls with that yellow telegram in his coat pocket on the back of the chair beside the bed that suddenly seemed to go around and around.

But when he closed his eyes, it stopped. He held his breath. He buried his head deeper in the pillows. He lay very still. It was dark and warm. And quiet, and darker than ever. A long time passed, a very long time, dark, and quiet, and peaceful, and still.

"Mr. Anderson! Hey, Mr. Anderson!"

In the darkness far off, somebody called, then nearer—but still very far away—then knocking on a distant door.

"Mr. Anderson!"

The voice was quite near now, sharper. The door opened, light streamed in. A hand shook his shoulder. He opened his eyes. Mrs. Dyer stood there, looking down at him in indignant amazement.

"Mr. Anderson, are you drunk?"

"No, Mrs. Dyer," he said in a daze, blinking at the land-lady standing above him. The electric light bulb she had switched on hurt his eyes.

"Mr. Anderson, they's a long-distance call for you on the phone down in the hall. Get up. Tie up that bathrobe. Hurry on down there and get it, will you? I've been yelling for you for five minutes."

"What time is it?" Carl sat bolt upright. The landlady stopped in the door.

"It's after dinnertime," she said. "Must be six-thirty, seven o'clock."

"Seven o'clock?" Carl gasped. "I've missed my bus!"

"What bus?"

"The four o'clock bus."

"I guess you have," said the landlady. "Alcohol and timetables don't mix, young man. That must be your mother on the phone now." Disgusted, she went down-stairs, leaving his door open.

The phone! Carl felt sick and unsteady on his legs. He pulled his bathrobe together and stumbled down the stairs. The phone! A kind of weakness rushed through his veins. The telephone! He had promised his mother not to drink. She said his father . . . He couldn't remember his father. He died long ago. Now his mother was . . . Anyhow, he should have been home by seven o'clock, at her bedside, holding her hand. He could have been home an hour ago. Now, maybe she . . .

He picked up the receiver. His voice was hoarse, fright-ened. "Hello. Yes, this is Carl . . . Yes, Mrs. Rossiter . . ."

"Carl, honey, we kept looking for you on that six o'clock bus. My husband went out on the road a piece to meet you in his car. We thought it might be quicker. Carl, honey . . ."

"Yes, Mrs. Rossiter . . ."

"Your mother . . ."

"Yes, Mrs. Rossiter . . ."

"Your mother just passed away. I thought maybe you ought to know in case you hadn't already started. I thought maybe . . ."

For a moment he couldn't hear what she said. Then he knew that she was asking him a question—that she was repeating it.

"I could have Jerry drive to Chicago and get you tonight. Would you like to have me do that, since there's no bus now until morning?"

"I wish you would, Mrs. Rossiter. But then, no—listen! Never mind! There's two or three things I ought to do before I come home. I ought to go to the bank. I must. But I'll catch that first bus home in the morning. First thing in the morning, Mrs. Rossiter, I'll be home."

"We're your neighbors and your friends. You know *this* is your home, too, so come right here."

"Yes, Mrs. Rossiter, I know. I will. I'll be home."

He ran back upstairs and jumped into his clothes, feeling that he had to get out. Had to get out! His body burned. His throat was dry. He picked up the wine bottle and looked at the label. Good wine! Warm and easy to the throat! Hurry before perhaps the landlady came. Hurry! She wouldn't understand this haste.

Did she die alone?

Quickly he put on his coat and plunged down the steps. Outside it was dark. The street lights seemed dimmer than usual.

Did she die alone?

At the corner, there was a bar, palely lighted. He had

never stopped there before, but this time he went in. He could drink all he wanted to now.

Alone, at home, alone! Did she die alone?

The bar was big and dismal, like a barn. A juke box played a raucous hit song. A woman stood near the machine singing to herself.

Carl went up to the bar.

"What'll it be?" The bartender passed his towel over the counter in front of him.

"A drink," Carl said.

"Whisky?"

"Yes."

"Can you make it two?" asked the woman in a warm low voice.

"Sure," Carl said. "Make it two."

"What's the matter? You're shivering!" she exclaimed.

"Cold," Carl said.

"You've been drinking?" the woman said. "But it don't smell like whisky."

"Wasn't," Carl said. "Was wine."

"Oh! I guess you can mix up your drinks, heh? O.K. Try it. But if that wine along with this whisky knocks you out," she purred, "I'll have to take you home to my house, little boy."

"Home?" Carl asked.

"Yes," the woman said, "home with me. You and me— home."

She put her arm around his shoulders.

"Home?" Carl said.

"Home, sure, baby! Home to my house."

"Home?" Carl was about to repeat when suddenly a volley of uncontrolled sobs shook his body, choking the word,

"Home." He leaned forward with his head in his arms and wept like a kid.

"Home. . . . . home . . . home . . . "

The bartender and the woman looked at him in amazement. The juke box stopped.

The woman said gently, "You're drunk, fellow. Come on, buck up! I'll take you home. It don't have to be to my house either—if you don't want to go. Where do you live? I'll see that you get home."

Mysterious Madame Shanghai

● *WE OTHER* roomers occasionally met her in the entrance hall, coming in or going out. She was a tall old woman. Her olive skin was leathery and seared, heavily lined, with the lines of her face and neck well-filled with a covering of rice powder. She spoke pleasantly enough in a deep, almost masculine voice, a simple, "Good day." That was all. But she never tried to make friends with any of the other roomers in the house. She was Mrs. Dyer's woman of mystery. Because she occasionally went down the second-floor hall to the bathroom in an amazing Chinese kimono of blue silk heavily brocaded with golden dragons, somebody had nicknamed her Madame Shanghai. The name stuck.

Mrs. Dyer, the landlady, certainly did not like her, and would wonder about her in a series of constantly varying and uncomplimentary suppositions—for nobody in the house really *knew* anything about Madame Shanghai. She looked like a gypsy, a fair East Indian, or a mulatto. But since she was no trouble and paid her rent on time, Mrs. Dyer had no good cause to ask her to move. Indeed, Mrs. Dyer did not honestly want her to move until she had wormed out of her who she was, had been, and why. Simply to know that her current name was Ethel Cunningham and that she worked now in the stock room of a downtown department store was really to know nothing at all—since it was written all over the woman that she had had a past.

Mrs. Dyer had great curiosity about her roomers' pasts. If they didn't have one, or failed to reveal it, our landlady usually made one up for them out of her own imagination, nourished by the novels she had read and the movies she had seen. The past which Mrs. Dyer created for Ethel Cunningham hardly became a lady.

"No woman could be so quiet today," Mrs. Dyer said to me one evening, "except that her morals've been loose in the past!"

I laughed, because I really didn't care about Madame Shanghai's morals, past or present. She was old enough to be my mother. So was Mrs. Dyer.

"Furthermore, no old woman would wear so much powder if she hadn't been used to wearing more when she was young!"

"Mrs. Dyer, could I have one of those big bath towels this week?"

"And forty years ago no nice girl covered up her complexion with rouge . . . . A big bath towel, you say? Them big towels is for my front rooms, young man. You don't occupy no walnut suite. How would them little towels of yours look hanging on a towel rack in them big rooms?"

"But I'm a big man, Mrs. Dyer, and I need a big towel to wipe myself on."

"Well, here—since it's to be drying yourself. Fact is, you are a pretty big fellow. But mind, you don't go putting your pal in the back room up to wanting a big towel, too. I haven't got but a dozen and they're for the front rooms, like I'm telling you."

"Yes, Mrs. Dyer. Thank you."

She waddled off down the hall. I gave her the polite raspberries—after I shut the door. Then I got out my clothes and started for the bathroom, but somebody was in there, so I came back, laid out a clean shirt on the bed and wiped off my tan shoes. When I finally got washed and dressed it was almost eight o'clock, a blue summer dusk, cool and pleasant. To take the girl to a show, or for a walk in the park? The park would be better, I thought, as I started down the dimly lighted steps in Mrs. Dyer's hall. At the curve of the stairs I almost ran over Ethel Cunningham. She was coming up very slowly, breathing heavily.

"Why, Madame Shang—Miss Cunningham," I stammered. She frightened me. "Are you sick?"

"I'm not sick—but– but—could you come upstairs with me, please a minute, Mr. Shields?"

"Let me help you."

I took her arm to the top of the steps and walked with her down the hall to her room. She fumbled nervously for her key, then opened the door. I had never been in her room before. It was a small room, not of the type to which Mrs. Dyer gave big towels. On the dresser were a number of photographs of a man—all the same man. In most of the pictures he wore a riding habit and carried a whip. He had a mustache. The pictures were faded, as though taken many years ago.

"That's him," Madame Shanghai gasped. "And he's waiting downstairs to kill me!"

"What?" I cried astonished, envisioning a man rushing into the room that very moment with drawn pistol.

"On the sidewalk," she said. "He hasn't seen me yet. But I saw him just as I started out."

I felt relieved that he had not seen her, but puzzled. Was she crazy?

"Go downstairs and tell him I love him," Madame Shanghai said, her eyes wide and anxious, her voice full of pleading. "Go tell him that God has punished me enough all these years."

"But what is it all about? I don't know what you mean. Who is he, Miss Cunningham?"

"My husband."

"Your husband?"

"Come back from the grave! I thought he was dead. I haven't seen him for twenty years—and then—now—oh, my God!" She sat on the bed and covered her face with her hands. "He was covered with blood."

"What?"

"I had tried to kill him. I let Tamaris tear the skin from his body and didn't even stop her."

"Tamaris?"

"The biggest cat in the world!"

"Cat?" I wanted to laugh because I thought she was talking about another woman.

"A tiger, Mr. Shields. I told Tamaris myself to claw him to death."

"But where did you get a tiger?"

She sat up and looked at me in surprise.

"Why, we were the greatest wild animal act in the business—before you were born, I guess. They billed us as the Daring Darnells. We played every circus and hippodrome in the world. But I was in love with him—too much in love—and jealous. He was in love with me, too—but cruel. Oh, so cruel! He thought *I* was an animal that needed to be tamed. So we fought all the time—with our fists, with whips, with our fingernails, with ropes. That was because we loved each other, I know now. I still love him. I want you to go downstairs and tell him I didn't mean to kill him. I'd go, but I'm afraid he'll shoot me before I get a chance to speak. Shoot me, or knife me, or slap my head off, I don't know which. He's a jealous man about women, Mr. Shields."

Again I wanted to laugh. Madame Shanghai was so wrinkled, ugly, and old, what man would want to knock her head off now?

"You tried to kill him once?"

"I thought I *had* killed him. I certainly wanted to. I sic'ed the wildest of the cats on him one night in the center of the big top before five thousand people. I thought he was dead when they dragged him out in front of a crowd sick with horror."

"Why did you try to kill him?"

"Over a ring, a ring my mother gave me, an old old ring with a hundred years of circus life behind it in Bohemia. That night, just as we went into the cage, Marie, the French bareback rider passed on her white horse leaving the arena, blowing kisses in answer to the applause—and there on her finger was my ring! I turned green with rage, jealousy, anger, hate. I knew my husband must have taken it from our trunk and given it to her to wear. She was beautiful and blonde—and he had a weakness for blonde women. I was dark as a gypsy. After I saw that ring on her finger, I said to him while we got the lions snarling into place on their stools, 'So you've stolen my ring and given it to that French hussy?'

" 'Shut up and take care of these cats,' was his answer. 'We're giving a performance.'

" 'I'll not shut up,' I said, 'you double-crossing no-good . . .'

"Just then the tigers leaped into the cage.

" 'My fist'll make you shut up as soon as I get out of this cage,' he said.

" 'You'll never get out,' I answered. 'Tamaris!'

"Tamaris was the largest and most beautiful of tigers, a tiger I had raised from a cub who obeyed me like a dog. I pointed my whip at the man in the ring whom I loved and hated more than anybody else in the world—my husband—whom I permitted to beat me, curse me, but whom I could not let give *my ring* to Marie.

" 'Tamaris!' I said, giving her the signal to spring.

"All the blood left my husband's face. Like lightning the sleek young animal crouched, then swept through the air. He screamed. Her great paws ripped into his flesh from the skull down. She bore him to the ground, mangled him with her tiger's teeth. The crowd gasped, sat tense, held its breath, then let loose a mighty groan of fright and horror as people saw the blood.

"From outside, the guards shot Tamaris. They opened the doors of the cage and took Jim out, a mass of bloody pulp. The show went on. They rushed him to the hospital. I walked back to the dressing tent. A dozen circus women crowded around to comfort me. But I wanted one thing only—that was my ring.

'The women were all astonished that I didn't cry. 'I can't cry,' I said. I was too humiliated, hurt, and angry. Just then Marie, that French woman, came in. I grabbed her hand, she thought for comfort, but really to see if my ring was there.

"Suddenly my heart stopped. It was *not* my ring, after all, on her finger! Merely one that looked like it! I could see it plainly now. The stone wasn't even the same kind of stone in her ring. It was paste.

"My blood turned to water. I stumbled across the tent to my trunk. I almost broke the lock. I could hardly wait to get it open. There, inside, safe as always, was my ring—the old gypsy ring of my mother's.

"Then I began to sob. I had deceived myself about my husband. I began to shriek. I howled like a mad woman. I tore my hair and rolled on the ground. Life can never hold another hour as bitter as that hour was for me.

"It was six weeks before Jim regained consciousness. The show went on across the country, but I remained behind by his side. When he opened his eyes at last and recognized me the first words he said were, 'Get away! Ethel, get away! Before I kill you.'

"The doctors would not allow me in the room with him after that. The sight of me sent him into a fury that endangered his life. The sound of my name caused him to burn with fever. I was forbidden to come into the hospital. So I went back to the circus. Always a great drawing card, as an animal tamer I was famous. I continued to make a great deal of money. I spent it all on my husband trying to bring him back to life and health—though he cursed me with every breath he drew into his slowly healing body. I knew that now for me from his scarred lips came nothing but hate. Still I sent him all the delicacies I could find that I thought he might like. I sent him champagne. I sent him money. I paid the hospital bills promptly. All he ever sent back was a curse or a threat, if he could persuade the doctors or nurses to write the profane words for him.

"Finally, without my knowledge, he was released from the hospital. I had wanted to see him to tell him I loved him, to beg his forgiveness on my knees, to devote the rest of my life to making him happy. I had hoped he would let me. Instead there came a wire from the head doctor at the hospital saying, 'Beware! He threatens to kill you.'

"And in a letter from his nurse that followed, I was told that he had spoken often of his intention to buy a gun, to trail the circus, to sit there in the audience some day and shoot me down as I stood in the center cage among my beautiful animals.

"Don't think, Mr. Shields, that I minded dying. It wasn't that. I simply did not want to die without a chance to speak to him, without a word of sorrow and love and apology for his ears. I wanted a chance to fall on my knees in front of him and say, 'Jim, forgive me.' Even though his gun was ready to blow my brains out.

"But to be shot without knowing when or where, without seeing Jim's face that I loved—even though mangled by tiger's claws and distorted with hate for me—to die without touching his hand even though it held my death! No! I couldn't bear that! Daily I went through hell after that letter came. Every time I entered the ring I expected a bullet to whistle out of the crowd. I lost control of my beasts. I went to pieces. I spent all my time in the cage peering into the crowd trying to see if he was there—my husband. Before my act I haunted the front of the big tent from noon on, looking to see if he entered the grounds. The managers thought I was going crazy. Though they liked freaks in the circus, they didn't like fools, so I gave up. I had to quit.

"I hid in a little town whose name I've forgotten now and let the circus go on without me. I let them have my animals. I changed my name. I worked as a cook, a maid, traveling everywhere looking for him, but I couldn't find him. Finally, I thought perhaps he had died. Then I came here to Chicago. Now, thank God, he's found me. But, oh, please, Mr. Shields, help me! Prepare him! Go downstairs and tell him not to kill me until I have a chance to say, 'Forgive me! Just forgive me. Jim, forgive me!' "

"I'll go," I said, still doubting, "and tell him—if he's still there."

"He'll never leave," the woman declared.

I went down the steps and out of Mrs. Dyer's rooming house, half smiling for I expected to see nobody on the sidewalk. I thought it was all just some crazy dream in Madame Shanghai's rice-powdered old head—but I was mistaken. Sure enough, in the half dark of the street lights just outside a man limped back and forth, a man bent sidewise as though by some old wound, an elderly man whose leather-colored face was crisscrossed by scars. His mouth was twisted. Now I was afraid, too.

"Pardon me," I said timidly, "but I've been told you are looking for a woman who lives in this house?"

"I am," he said, "since you seem to know. I'm looking for my wife."

"To—to—kill her?" I asked.

He said nothing.

"She wants to speak to you before you do," I said.

"Then tell her to come to me," he answered.

"You'll give her a chance?"

"Tell her to come and see."

I went back into the house and told her what he had said.

"I'll go," she answered. I was trembling, but she was not.

Madame Shanghai went bravely down the steps walking like a woman used to going into a cage with wild animals. I followed her to the door, cold sweat on my forehead. Already, as if in anticipation of drama, three or four people had gathered on the sidewalk. Mrs. Dyer had raised her window.

The man in the street waited quite still for his wife to come toward him beneath the street light. She went, holding out her arms in a gesture of the greatest love I have ever seen. But then she swayed, put her hands to her mouth, called weakly, "Jim!" and fell in a faint at his feet.

The man with the crooked body hesitated, then bent down swiftly and lifted her in his arms. He came up the steps into the house.

"Where is her room?" he asked.

I pointed upward. He went ahead and I followed, trailed now by a half-dozen roomers. He burst in through the half-open door and laid her on the bed. As he bent over a pistol fell from his pocket. But he did not pick it up.

"You are not going to kill her?" I said.

"No," he answered tensely, "I'm just going to slap the life back into her . . . then I'm going to kiss her."

He began to slap her face soundly on one cheek, then the other, and a dusty haze of rice powder floated upward.

Madame Shanghai opened her eyes. "Jim!" she cried, "you love me—or you wouldn't be slapping me like this. You love me! You love me!"

They kissed, crushed in each other's arms. We closed their door, but it was hard to get our landlady out of the hall.

● *Never Room with a Couple*

● *EVEN* if they don't pay very much, you can have lots of fun working in a summer camp and you meet plenty of funny people. Last summer at a big camp in upstate New York I was head chief dishwasher and bottle-wiper, with plenty else to do besides. For one thing, I had to help the cook get all the vegetables ready. I peeled so many potatoes that if you'd put all them spuds eye to eye they'd reach from Waycross to Jalapy and back. But who's gonna worry 'bout that? Summer's gone now.

One afternoon me and the second cook was sitting out in the shade behind the cook shack peeling spuds, when up from the lake comes a Jewish couple quarreling to beat the band. They was in bathing suits, a man and his wife, and they was both kinda fat and old. When they quarreled their stomachs wobbled up and down. I wanted to laugh, but I didn't.

"You see that?" said the second cook. "I bet she's been flirtin' underwater with some other man."

"Might be the other way round," I said. "Maybe it was him and another woman."

"Which ever way it was," said the cook, "some woman is to blame."

"What makes you figger that?" I asked.

"It's always a woman is to blame," said the cook as he grabbed a potato I had just peeled, and looked at me. "Pick out them eyes good, boy," he said, although I knew perfectly well how to peel potatoes and *was* picking out the eyes good. But then I was only eighteen and Allie was an old guy about forty, always giving me advice. He sort of took it upon himself to look out for me, so he was always telling me stories with morals, like I was a kid.

"I never will forget that last family quarrel I was mixed up in," Allie went on as we peeled and cut. "Who was to blame? A woman! Son, they's terrible! That hussy like to ruint me!"

"Who?" I said. "Where? When?"

"Never room with a couple," Allie counseled gravely. He paused to let this warning sink in. "Son, as long as you away from your mother's home, no matter where you may be, never room with a married couple. It's dangerous!" He looked me solemnly in the eye over our bucket of potatoes. "You are young and you don't know! But, boy, I'm tellin' you, if you rent a room when you go back to Harlem, rent from a widow or an orphan, a West Indian or a Geechee, but never room with a couple! A man and his wife, plus a roomer—son, that's poison!"

"Why?" I said to keep the tale going and get the potatoes peeled so I could take a swim before supper.

"Why?" Allie answered, looking at me as if I was a child. "I'm gonna tell you why. Look at me, here peeling potatoes! Well, I used to be a first-class captain-waiter who could carry more orders on one tray than any waiter in New York—and look at me now! All from roomin' with a couple."

"What!" I said in astonishment.

"Sure, just look at me!" Allie said. "Their name was Wilkins. A nice young couple, Joe and his wife, Fannie. I used to run on the road with Joe before I quit the dining cars. So when he told me one day, 'Me and my wife's got a nice little apartment in 143rd. Why don't you come on up and room with us, fellow? Quiet and homelike—and only three bucks a week,' I said, 'I believe I will.' Which I did, cause I knowed they needed the rent. So long about this time last year I moved in and paid my rent. They gimme the rear back room. They had a nice apartment on the third floor, with my window looking across the alley at more third floors. Nighttime, all them radios goin', it was swell! Harlem just full o' music—not like up here in these woods where all you can hear is yourself snorin'."

"Then what happened?" I said.

"Funny thing, son," Allie went on. "Before I went there to room, Joe's wife ain't never appealed to me a-tall. I like 'em three-quarters pink, and she were just a ordinary light brown-skin. But seemed like to me Fannie blossomed out and got prettier after I moved in. Or maybe seein' her every day at close range got me used to overlookin' her fizziogomy. Anyhow, one Sunday morning when Joe's train was out and I was goin' to the bath to shave, I met her trippin' down the hall on her way to church. I said, 'Baby, I could go for you!' When Fannie flashed them pearly teeth o' her'n in my face, I said, 'When do Joe come home?'

"She said, 'Not till twelve o'clock tonight.'

"I said, 'That'll do!' And, son, don't you know that woman got crazy about me?"

"Naturally," I answered, sarcastic-like, because in every tale he told, the women were always crazy about him.

Allie went on, "Fannie wanted to give me a diamond ring, but I wouldn't take it. I said, 'No, honey, your husband's just a working man.'

"She said, 'That don't make no difference, Allie. I'd take Joe's money and buy *you* a diamond—just to see you smile.'

"But I said, 'No, baby, I really don't need nary diamond. Just let me wear somethin' o' your'n. Any old thing —to think of you by!'

"She said, 'What?'

"I said, 'How about that little old horseshoe ring you got on your finger there?'

"She said, 'Aw, no, sugar! That belongs to Joe. He lets me wear it, but it ain't no good.'

"So I said, 'You thinks more of Joe than you does of me?'

" 'No, I don't, honey!' she said real quick. 'You can have it, if you want it. Here!' And she gimme Joe's ring. 'But don't wear it around the house,' she said.

" 'Do you think I'm a fool?' I told her.

"I really didn't want the ring nohow, but I knowed it was Joe's—and I just wanted to see would she give it to me. Well, sir, to make a long story short, it wasn't no time till Joe found out that that ring was gone. Then it was that I should've moved, but I didn't have the sense—not thinkin' he'd suspicion *me*. We was always such good friends on the road.

"But one night I come home from the hotel where I was workin' and I'd no more than put my key in the latch when I heard 'em quarrelin'. I tipped down the hall real easy past their bedroom door, but when I went to unlock my own door, since I had done left my window open in the morning, the wind blew the door back with a bang. I heard Joe open his door and say, 'There's that so-and-so now!' So I knew they was quarrelin' 'bout me!

" 'Baby,' Fannie said to Joe, 'come in here and shut the door. Can't you see I ain't got no clothes on?'

" 'Shut up!' said Joe, and he called her out of her name.

" 'Don't call me that,' said Fannie, 'cause I'm a pure woman.'

" 'You don't say!' said Joe.

" '*Say*, nothin', Joe Wilkins,' she hollered, 'you know I am,' said Fannie.

" 'Yes, until that roomer come here,' yelled Joe. 'Right up till last August when Allie King showed up?'

" 'Till now, as far as Allie is concerned,' yelled Fannie.

" 'Then where is my horseshoe ring?'

" 'In the drawer,' she lied.

" 'Lemme see!'

"I could hear Fannie lookin' through the drawers for that ring she knew wasn't there—cause I had it in my pocket. Then she begins to cry—and I was sweatin' blood! I ain't even turned on the light yet in my room. Just holdin' my hat in my hand *sweatin' blood*—cause there wasn't but one way to get out of my room without passin' their door, and that was to jump. The third floor is pretty high—but Joe's a fightin' man.

" 'Fannie,' he said, 'who's got my ring?'

" 'What do you mean, who?' cried Fannie.

" 'You know what *who* means,' said Joe.

" 'Somebody must-a stole it,' said Fannie.

" 'Who'd steal a no-good horseshoe ring?' said Joe. 'You give it to Allie King.'

" 'Ow-o-o-o-o-o!' cried Fannie. I knowed he'd raised his hand to hit her—so I put on my hat to go.

" 'And you ain't the only one I'm gonna hit,' yelled Joe. 'I'm goin' in there and beat that no-good son-of-a-so-and-so to death right now.' He started down the hall for me.

" 'Aw-ooo-oo-o!' Fannie yelled as I heard Joe chargin' towards my door—but before he could put his hand on the knob, I was gone!"

"Gone where?" I asked, dropping a potato.

"Gone out," said Allie. "I stepped right through that third-floor window down into the yard."

"Three stories down?"

"I didn't miss it," said Allie. "I like to took that window with me, too—I was in such a hurry. Don't think I lingered in the back yard neither. No, sir! I crawled right on up to Lenox and grabbed me a taxi."

"Crawled?" I said.

"Sure, *crawled!* I'd done broke both my ankles! That's why I'm peelin' spuds out here in this lonesome camp today. I can't wait table no mo' with these crippled-up feet—and all from roomin' with a couple!"

Allie looked at me with a warning eye over our bucket of potatoes.

"*Never* room with a couple, son," he said solemnly, "less'n they are over eighty."

● *Little Old Spy*

● *A NUMBER* of years ago, toward the end of one of Cuba's reactionary regimes, on the evening of my second day in Havana, I realized I was being followed. I had walked too far for the same little old man, trailing a respectable distance behind me, to be there accidentally. I noticed him first standing quite close to me when I stopped to buy a paper at the big newsstand across from the Alhambra. He seemed to be trying to see what I was buying.

Then I forgot about him. I walked down the Prado in the warm dusk looking at the American tourists on parade, watching the fine cars that passed, and seeing the lights catch fire from the sunset. When I got to the bandstand by the fort at the waterfront, I stopped, leaned against the wall, and put my foot out for a ragged little urchin to shine. I was lighting a cigarette when the little old man of the newsstand strolled by in front of me. He stopped a few paces beyond, and called a boy to shine his shoes. Even then I thought nothing of his being there. But I did notice his strange get-up, the tight suit, the cream-colored spats, and the floppy panama with its bright band that a youth, but not an old man, could have worn. He was a queer little withered Cuban, certainly sixty years old, but dressed like a fop of twenty.

A mile away on the Malecon—for I had continued to walk along the sea wall—I looked at my watch and saw the hour approaching seven, when I was to meet some friends at the Florida Café. I turned to retrace my steps. In turning, whom should I face on the sidewalk but the little old man! Then I became suspicious. He said nothing, and strolled on as though he had not seen me. But when I looked back after walking perhaps a quarter mile toward the center, there he was, a respectable distance behind.

Later that evening at the restaurant, midway through the salad, I noticed him alone at a far table sipping coffee and looking sort of out of place in the fashionable dining room.

"Say, who is that fellow?" I asked my friend, the newspaper editor, as we sat with his cousin, the poet, and a little dancer named Mata. Carlos, the editor, looked across the restaurant toward the table I indicated.

"Don't everybody look," I said as Mata and Jorge began bending their necks, too. "It might embarrass him."

But when Carlos turned his head toward us again and answered in a whispering voice, "A spy," none of us could keep our eyes from glancing quickly across the café.

"What?" I said.

"Yes," Carlos affirmed, "a government spy."

"But why should he be following me?" I asked.

"He has been following you?"

"All afternoon."

"Maybe he thinks you're Communist," Carlos said. "That's what they are afraid of here."

"But they've got a lot more to be afraid of than that," Jorge added.

"I guess they have," I answered, for everybody knew Cuba was on the verge of a revolution. All the schools were closed, and the public buildings guarded. The "they" we so discreetly referred to meant the government and the tyrant at its head. But nobody mentioned the tyrant's name in public; and nobody talked very loud, if they talked at all.

For months there had been political murders in the streets of the capital, riots in the provinces, and American gunboats in the harbors. Mobs were becoming bolder and bolder, crying in public places, "Down with the Yankees! Down with the government that supports them!" But the tourists seemed blissfully unaware of all this. They still flocked to the Casino, wore their fine clothes through quaint streets of misery, danced nightly rhumbas at the big hotels, and took tours into the countryside, exclaiming before the miserable huts of the sugar-cane cutters, "How picturesque! How cute!"

"Yes," went on Carlos (this time in English), pouring a beer. "He ees spy. I know heem. On newspaper you know everybody. But he ees no dangerous."

"Not dangerous?" I said.

"Not, joust a poor little *viejo*, once pimp, now spy."

"Oh," I said.

"But tomorrow the government will know with whom you dined," said Mata, "and that maybe will be dangerous."

"Why?" I asked.

"To dine with anyone in Havana is dangerous," Jorge laughed, "unless it is with the big boss himself. Everybody else, except the police, are against the government. And that paper of my cousin's," indicating Carlos, "*Caramba!* It has been suppressed ten times."

"But I thought it was your best paper."

"It is—but they think they are our *best* government."

Just then the waiter came bringing more beer. We switched our conversation into Spanish again and the domestic troubles of the Pickford-Fairbanks ménage—then of great interest to the readers of Carlos' paper.

"But what shall I do about the spy?" I asked, when the waiter had gone. "I never imagined such open spying."

"They are that way down here," Carlos said. "Not very subtle."

"Make friends with him," suggested Jorge, eating a *flan*. "That would be amusing."

"Buy heem a few drinks," said Carlos, "I know his kind. All they looking for, after all, ees easiest way to get few drinks. The government ees full of drunkards."

Meanwhile the little spy kept mournfully sipping his coffee across the room. Evidently his allowance for spying called for nothing better than coffee when his job took him into an expensive restaurant. I pitied him sitting there looking at all the good food going by and getting nothing.

"Say," I said to Carlos and Jorge, "won't it be dangerous for you and Mata, sitting here with me—if I'm suspected of being a dangerous man."

"To sit with anybody is dangerous in Havana," Jorge replied. "But they can't lock up everyone. Or kill all of us. After all, it is not writers like my cousin and me that they are really afraid of. Or visiting dancers like Mata. No, it is the workers. You see, they can stop refineries from running. They can keep ships from being loaded, and sugar cane from being cut. They can hit in the pocketbook—and that's all our damned government's here for—to protect foreign dividends."

"Sure, I know that," I said. "But why's that man watching me?"

"Because strangers who don't at once make for the Casino to start gambling are watched. *Poor* strangers may be sympathetic with our revolution. They may be bearers of messages from our group in exile. That's why they watch you."

"But if you want heem to forget all about it, buy heem few drinks," shrugged Carlos. "We kill all their best spies. We don't bother with little old bums like heem. Bullets too valuable."

The little man across the way took out a pack of cheap cigarettes and began to smoke. Carlos, Mata, Jorge, and I sat talking until almost midnight. Well-dressed Americans and portly Cubans passed and repassed between the tables. A famous Spanish actress came in with her man on her arm. There was music somewhere at the back of the café, and talk, laughter, and clatter of dishes everywhere. We stopped thinking about the spy and began to speak of Mayakovsky—for Jorge, who was putting his verse into Spanish, declared him the greatest poet of the twentieth century, but Carlos disagreed in favor of Lorca, so a discussion sprang up.

When I left my friends, the little brown man was right at my heels. He trailed behind me until I finally got into a taxi. As the car drew off, I knew he was taking down the license number. Later the police would find out from the chauffeur where I had been driven.

I was not a little flattered to be so assiduously spied upon. At home in Harlem I was nobody, just a Negro writer. Down here in Havana I was suddenly of governmental importance. And I knew pretty well why. The government of Cuba had grown suddenly terribly afraid of its Negro population, its black shine boys and cane field hands, its colored soldiers and sailors who make up most of the armed forces, its taxi drivers and street vendors. At last, after all the other elements of the island's population had openly revolted against the tyrant in power, the Negroes had begun to rise with the students and others to drive the dictator from Cuba.

For a strange New York Negro to come to Havana might mean—*quién sabe?*—that he had come to help stir them up—for the Negroes of Harlem were reputed in Cuba to be none too docile, and none too dumb. Had not Marcus Garvey come out of Harlem to arouse the whole black world to a consciousness of its potential strength?

"They," the Cuban dictatorship, were afraid of Negroes from Harlem. The American steamship lines at that time would not sell colored persons tickets to Cuba. The immigration at the port of Havana tried to keep them out, if they got that far. But here was I—and I was being shadowed.

The next day I went downstairs to breakfast in the café-bar of my hotel. The iron shutters were up and the whole front of the building open to the street, dust, and sunshine.

Across the way in a Spanish wineshop, I saw the little old man of the day before waiting patiently.

"Today," I thought to myself, "we will make friends. There ought to be an amusing story in you, old top, if I can get it out."

But after breakfast, for the fun of it, I gave him a merry chase first. By streetcar, by taxi, on foot, down narrow old streets and up broad new ones, all over the central part of Havana, he trotted after me. I had a number of errands to do and I did them in as zigzag a manner as possible. Once I lost him. But just as I was beginning to regret it (for the game was not unamusing), I looked around and there, not ten feet away from me in El Centro, was the little old man, puffing and blowing to be sure, but nevertheless there. I laughed. But the sweating little spy did not seem to find the situation entertaining. One of his spats had become unbuttoned from running, and his watch chain was hanging.

That afternoon I had tea with Señora Barrios, the Chilean novelist, my spy waiting patiently the while outside the hedge of her Vedado villa. No taxi being in sight when I emerged, I walked along toward the center of the city, giving the old man some exercise.

On a quiet corner near the statue of Gomez, I sighted a little bar and went across for a drink before dinner. My withered dandy stood forlornly without.

"It'll be fun to tire him," I thought. "I'll sit here drinking nice cool beers until he can stand it no longer and will have to come in, too. Then I'll invite him to have a drink and see what happens."

It worked. The little old man could not forever stand on that corner and watch me drinking comfortably within. I knew his throat was dry. At last he entered, wiping his brow, and called for an anisette at the small bar.

"Have a Bacardi with me," I invited. "I don't like to drink alone."

The little old man started, stared, seemed hesitant as to whether he should answer at all or not, and finally slid into the chair across from my own. The waiter brought us two drinks and put them on the marble-topped table.

"Hot," I said pleasantly.

"*Sí, señorito*, like steam," the little old man answered.

"You've been walking quite a lot, too," I laughed.

"Too much for my age," the old man said. "You Americanos are *muy activo*. That's no good in this climate."

"Have another drink," I said.

The old man accepted with alacrity. Just as Carlos said, he loved his Bacardi. He smiled and nodded as I called the waiter.

"Say," I said, "you have a hell of a job."

"I know it," he said, "but, señorito, I took it to keep out of jail."

"How come," I asked, "jail?"

"A woman," he said, "they had me for cutting a woman. I caught her giving her money to some other man after all I did for her, so I nearly killed her."

"Aren't you pretty old for that girl-racket, señor?"

"Not too old to knife one if she crosses me. They had me in jail locked up. But I said to them, I'm no good here, not to you nor me either. I know languages, I know people,

I'm smart—so the Porra turned me out to help them scent revolutionists. Now they've switched me to the foreign squad. I get two dollars a day for just running around behind you. 'They' don't like strange foreigners."

We were speaking in Spanish, but when I switched to English he understood me equally well.

He spoke the English of the wharf rats and the bad Spanish of one who wants to speak Castilian. He was provincial and grandiloquent. But when he began to speak of women, as he did shortly, he was poetical too.

For years he had been a procurer on the waterfront, I learned as we drank. Even to his own wife, when he had one, he would bring lovers from among the sailors. The crumpled bills in his hand, the round silver dollars, meant more to him than any woman could ever mean, I gathered from his talk.

That afternoon he was quite out of breath from trailing me. He needed to rest, drink, sit, and talk to somebody. I was interested, so I began to ask him questions as I kept his glass filled.

"Those women," I said, "that you exploited, didn't they care?"

"Couldn't care," he said. "Most of 'em are poor, some of 'em are black, all of 'em loved me. They couldn't afford to care. Without me they might have died, anyhow. I looked out for them. Man, when I was young, the money they brought me! Whew-oo-o!"

As he told his story, I discovered that the little brown man was the very essence of those people who want a good time in life—and don't care how they get it. He had no morals. He had no qualms about using for gain the women who loved him or sought his protection. But, as he grew older, naturally they sought the favors of younger men;

new kings arose in the brothels. Then he took to intimi-
dations, to knives and beatings to hold his power. When
he could no longer pay off the police, they put him in jail,
so he became a spy.

"Drink," I said.

"*Sí, señor.*"

As he put his glass down, he twirled his little wax mustache and looked at me across the marble table in the
darkening café. Outside the street lights had come on and
the tropical evening deepened into night.

"Come, let us go to San Isidro Street, señorito," said
the little man. "Along about now the girls are coming out."

"What's there," I asked, "in San Isidro Street?"

"Just women," said the little man, "of the waterfront."

"Pretty?" I asked.

"Yes," said the little man, "very pretty."

"So!" I said. "Have a drink."

This time I asked the waiter to bring a whole bottle of
rum and leave it on our table. As the little man partook, he
became more and more grandiloquent on the subject of
women.

"The women of Cuba," he said, "are like the pome-
granates of Santa Clara. Their souls are jeweled, *joven*,
their blood is red, their lips are sweet. And sweetest of all
are the mulattoes of Camagüey, *Americanito*. They are
the sweetest of all."

"Why the mulattoes?" I said.

"Because," said the old man, "they are a mixture of two
worlds, two extremes, two bloods. You see, señorito, the
passion of the blacks and the passion of the whites com-
bine in the smoldering heat that is *la mulata*. The
rose of Venus blooms in her body. She's pain and she's
pleasure. You see, señorito, I know. In the pure Negro,

soul and body are separate. In the white they work badly together. But in the mulatto they strangle each other—and their strangulation produces that sweet juice that is a yellow woman's love."

With this amazing observation the little brown man, once a merchant in bodies, lifted his glass of rum and drank. He swayed a little in his chair as he put the glass down. He looked at me with funny far-off eyes. "I wish I were young again," he said. "Come, let's go down to San Isidro Street, sonny."

"Alright, wait a minute."

I got up and left the table. The little brown man's head was in his arms when I looked back. His eyes were closed. I slipped the barman a bill and went out, leaving more than half a bottle of Bacardi on the table.

That night I delivered all the messages that the exiles in the Latin-American quarter of Harlem had sent by me to their revolutionary co-workers in Havana.

On the boat to New York two days later, off the coast of Georgia, the wireless brought the news that the Cuban government was falling, and that a "pack of Negresses from the waterfront had torn the clothes off the backs of a party of cabinet wives as they came to visit their husbands in jail."

I wonder, I thought to myself, what the women of San Isidro Street would have done to that withered little old man had I gone there with him that night and whispered to them that he was a spy? They probably would have torn him to pieces and given his gold watch chain to some younger man. On the end of the chain I felt sure he had no watch.

● *Tragedy at the Baths*

●   "*THAT* it should happen in my Baths!" was all she could say. "That it should happen in my Baths!" And try as they would, nobody could console her.

165

Señora Rueda was quite hysterical. Being a big strong woman, her screams alarmed the neighborhood.

She and her now-deceased husband had owned the Baths for years—the Esmeralda Baths—among the cleanest and most respectable in Mexico City, family baths where only decent people came for their weekly tub or shower or *baño de vapor*. Indeed, her establishment, with its tiled courtyard and splashing fountain, was a monument to the neighborhood, a middle-class section of flats and shops near the Loreto. Now this had happened!

Why! Señora Rueda had known the young man for years—that is, he had been a customer of the Esmeralda Baths since his youth, coming there for his weekly shower and swim in the little tiled tank. Sometimes, when he was flush, he took a private tub, and a good steaming out— which cost a *peso*. Juan Maldonado was the young man's name. He was a tall nice-looking boy.

That Sunday morning when he presented himself at the wicket and asked for a private tub for two—himself and his wife—Señora Rueda was not especially surprised. Even by reading the papers, one can't keep up with all the marriages that take place—and young men will eventually get married.

As she handed Juan his change she looked up to see beside him a vibrant black-haired girl with the soft Indian-brown complexion of a Mexican *mestiza*. Señora Rueda smiled. A nice couple, she thought as the attendant showed them to their room and their tub. Two beautiful youths, she thought, and sighed.

Some bathhouses, she knew, did not allow the sexes to mingle within their walls, but Señora Rueda did not mind when they were legally married. Being respectable neighborhood baths, nothing but decent people were her patrons, anyway. She had no reason to suspect young Maldonado.

But an hour later there was another tale to tell! Not even smelling salts then could calm poor Señora Rueda. Oh, why did it have to happen in her Baths? *Por dios*, why?

This is the story as it came to me. It may not be wholly true for, in the patios and courtyards of Loreto, romantic and colorful additions have probably been added by those who know Juan and his family. The Mexicans love sad, romantic tales with many embroidered touches of sentimental heartbreak and ironic frustration. But, although versions of what led up to that strange Sunday morning in the Esmeralda Baths may vary in the telling, what actually happened therein—everybody knows. And it was awful!

In the first place, they were not married, Juan and that woman!

He met her in a very strange way, anyhow. The mounted police were charging a demonstration against the government. The Zocalo was filled with people trampling the grass and the flowers. Juan crossed the square on the way to the shop where he worked, giving the demonstrators a wide berth—as his particular politics were not involved that day. But just as he got midway across the Zocalo, the police began to charge on horses and the crowd began to run, so Juan was forced to run, too.

Everyone was trying to reach the shelter of the *portales* opposite the Palace, or the gates of the Cathedral, or the safety of a side street. Juan was heading toward Avenida Madero, the clatter of the horses' hoofs behind him when, just in front of him, a woman stumbled and fell.

Juan stopped running and picked her up, lifted her in his arms and went on. Once out of the square, in the quiet

of a side street, he put her down on her feet and offered her
his handkerchief to wipe the dust and tears from her face.
Then he saw that she was young and very beautiful with
the soft Indian-brown complexion of a Mexican mestiza.

"Ay, Señor," she said to the tall young man in front of
her, "how can I ever thank you?"

But just at that moment a man approached, hatless and
wild-eyed. He, too, had been caught in the spinning
crowd, had seen his wife fall, but could not get to her—and
then she had disappeared! For a while, the husband was
frantic, but finally he caught sight of her around the corner
faced by a tall young man who was offering her his handkerchief and gazing deep into her lovely eyes.

"You don't need to thank me," the young man was saying, "just let me look at you," as the girl caught sight of her
approaching husband.

"Sunday at the Maximo," she whispered. "I want to
thank you alone."

"At your service," said the young man, as the panting
husband arrived.

Now, the husband was also a fairly young man, but
neither as tall nor as handsome as Maldonado. He was much
too short and frail to be married to so charming a woman.
He kept an *escritorio*, a writing room, in the Portal of
Santo Domingo on the little square, where letters were
written for peasants who had no education, and where people could get legal documents copied on the typewriter, or
have their names penned with decorative flourishes on a
hundred calling cards.

The husband, too, there in the side street that day,
thanked young Maldonado for having rescued his wife
from the feet of the crowd and the hoofs of the police
horses. Then they all shook hands and went their way, the

tall young man going south, the pretty girl and her prosaic husband north.

But the following Sunday Maldonado waited at the entrance of the Cinema Maximo, where a Bogart film was being shown, and about five o'clock, sure enough, she appeared, alone. She was even prettier than the day he had picked her up in the Zocalo, and very shy, as if ashamed of what she was doing.

They took seats way up in the balcony, where lovers sit and hold hands in the dark. And soon they were holding hands, too.

"There was something about the strength of your arms the other day," she said, "even before I looked into your eyes, that made me want to stay with you forever."

"Stop!" yelled a cop, firing across the screen.

"And there was something in the feel of your body lying in my arms that made me never want to put you down," said Juan.

"My name is Consuelo Aguilar," the girl said softly. "You have met my husband."

"Tell me about him," said Juan.

"He is crazy about me," Consuelo answered, "and terribly jealous! He wants to be a writer, but all he writes is letters for peasants."

"And if he knew you were here—?"

"But he won't know. He stays home on Sundays and writes poems! When I tell him they're no good, he says I don't love him and threatens to commit suicide. He is very emotional, my little husband."

"And where does he think you are now?"

"At my aunt's."

It was really love, and at first sight, so they say in the

patios of Loreto. But they also say that Juan was a little dumb, and a little inexperienced in the ways of women.

They kept on meeting in *cines* and dance halls, and things began to be more and more dangerous for both of them, for husbands very often kill lovers in Mexico—and go free. It is the thing to do! But what this husband did was even worse! At least, Señora Rueda thought so.

But what his wife did was terrible, too. In Catholic lands where divorces are practically impossible, and where women are never supposed to leave their husbands, any-how—this wife planned to run away with Maldonado! But, being young and foolish (or so they say in Loreto), for some strange reason or other, on the Sunday of their elopement, they planned to take a bath first. And that is how the couple happened to be in Señora Rueda's quiet Esmeralda Baths.

There the husband came and caught them! Or, rather, he deliberately followed them there. The miracle was that he did not kill them both! Instead, he bought a season's ticket for a whole year of baths (probably not realizing what he was doing) then went into the corridor outside the room where Juan and Consuelo were bathing—and shot *himself!*

Then it was that the uproar began, and such an uproar! People commenced to emerge from their tubs, clad and unclad, to run and scream. Doors began to open, and steam escaped into the courtyard. In the excitement, some-one turned off the water main and the fountain stopped running. Naturally, Consuelo and Maldonado came out to see what was going on—and stumbled over the bleeding body of Señor Aguilar at their feet.

"Oh, my God!" Consuelo cried. "He said he would kill himself if I ran away with you."

"How did he ever know you were coming away with *me?*" asked the young man in astonishment.

"I told him," said Consuelo. Her eyes were hard. "I wanted to see if he really would commit suicide. He threatened to so often. But now, darling," she turned softly toward Juan, "with him gone, we can get married."

"But suppose he had killed *us!*" said Maldonado, trembling in the doorway with only a towel about his body.

"That little coward," sneered Consuelo, "wasn't man enough!"

"But he did kill himself," said Maldonado slowly, turning back into the room away from the body on the floor and the crowd that had gathered.

"Kiss me," purred Consuelo, lifting her pretty face toward Juan's, as she closed their door.

"Get away from me!" cried Juan, suddenly sickened with horror. Flinging open the door, he gave her a terrific push into the hall.

Consuelo fell prone over the body of her husband and, beginning to realize that she was, after all, a widow, and that there were six good typewriters to be inherited from the escritorio, she commenced to sob in approved fashion on the floor, embracing the corpse of her late spouse, hysterically—as a good wife should.

When the police got through asking questions of them both, and of Señora Rueda, Juan went home alone and left Consuelo still crying at the Baths It took him a long time to get over the fact that she had told her husband—and the sound of that single pistol shot echoed in his head for months.

But the saddest thing of all, so they say in Loreto, was that when the details of their tragic triangle appeared in the papers, Juan's employer read them with such scandalized interest that he promptly dismissed him from his work. Consuelo lost only a husband she didn't want. But young Maldonado lost his *job*.

As for Señora Rueda, she swore never to rent another tub to a couple.

● *Trouble with the*
Angels

● *AT EVERY* performance lots of white people wept. And almost every Sunday while they were on tour some white minister invited the Negro actor who

173

played God to address his congregation and thus help improve race relations—because almost everywhere they needed improving. Although the play had been the hit of the decade in New York, its Negro actors and singers were paid much less than white actors and singers would have been paid for performing it. And, although the white producer and his backers made more than half a million dollars, the colored troupers on tour lived in cheap hotels and often slept in beds that were full of bugs. Only the actor who played God would sometimes, by the hardest, achieve accommodations in a white hotel, or be put up by some nice white family, or be invited to the home of the best Negroes in town. Thus God probably thought that everything was lovely in the world. As an actor he really got very good write-ups in the papers.

Then they were booked to play Washington, and that's where the trouble began. Washington, the capital of the United States is, as every Negro knows, a town where no black man was allowed inside a downtown theater, not even in the gallery until very recently. The legitimate playhouses had no accommodations for colored people. Incredible as it may seem, until Ingrid Bergman made her stand, Washington was worse than the Deep South in that respect.

But God wasn't at all worried about playing Washington. He thought surely his coming would improve race relations. He thought it would be fine for the good white people of the Capital to see him—a colored God—even if Negroes couldn't. Not even those Negroes who worked for the government. Not even the black Congressman.

But several weeks before the Washington appearance of the famous "Negro" play about charming darkies who drank eggnog at a fish fry in heaven, storm clouds began to rise. It seemed that the Negroes of Washington strangely enough had decided that they, too, wanted to see this play. But when they approached the theater management on the question, they got a cold shoulder. The management said they didn't have any seats to sell Negroes. They couldn't even allot a corner in the upper gallery—there was such a heavy ticket demand from white folks.

Now this made the Negroes of Washington mad, especially those who worked for the government and constituted the best society. The teachers at Howard got mad, too, and the ministers of the colored churches who wanted to see what a black heaven looked like on the stage.

But nothing doing! The theater management was adamant. They really couldn't sell seats to Negroes. Although they had no scruples about making a large profit on the week's work of Negro actors, they couldn't permit Negroes to occupy seats in the theater.

So the Washington Negroes wrote directly to God, this colored God who had been such a hit on Broadway. They thought surely he would help them. Several organizations, including the Negro Ministerial Alliance, got in touch with him when he was playing Philadelphia. What a shame, they said by letter, that the white folks will not allow us to come to see you perform in Washington. We are getting up a protest. We want you to help us. Will you?

Now God knew that for many years white folks had not allowed Negroes in Washington to see any shows—not even in the churches, let alone in theaters! So how come they suddenly thought they ought to be allowed to see God in a white playhouse?

Besides, God was getting paid pretty well, and was pretty well known. So he answered their letters and said that although his ink was made of tears, and his heart bled, he couldn't afford to get into trouble with Equity. Also, it wasn't his place to go around the country spreading dissension and hate, but rather love and beauty. And it would surely do the white folks of the District of Columbia a lot of good to see Him, and it would soften their hearts to hear the beautiful Negro spirituals and witness the lovely black angels in his play.

The black drama lovers of Washington couldn't get any real satisfaction out of God by mail—their colored God. So when the company played Baltimore, a delegation of the Washington Negroes went over to the neighboring city to interview him. In Baltimore, Negroes, at least, were allowed to sit in the galleries of the theaters.

After the play, God received the delegation in his dressing room and wept about his inability to do anything concerning the situation. He had, of course, spoken to his management about it and they thought it might be possible to arrange a special Sunday night performance for Negroes. God said it hurt him to his soul to think how his people were mistreated, but the play must go on.

The delegation left in a huff—but not before they had spread their indignation to other members of the cast of the show. Then among the angels there arose a great discussion as to what they might do about the Washington situation. Although God was the star, the angels, too, were a part of the play.

Now, among the angels there was a young Negro named Johnny Logan who never really liked being an angel, but who, because of his baritone voice and Negro features, had gotten the job during the first rehearsals in New York. Now, since the play had been running three years, he was an old hand at being an angel.

Logan was from the South—but he hadn't stayed there

long after he grew up. The white folks wouldn't let him. He was the kind of young Negro most Southern white people hate. He believed in fighting prejudice, in bucking against the traces of discrimination and Jim Crow, and in trying to knock down any white man who insulted him. So he was only about eighteen when the whites ran him out of Augusta, Georgia.

He came to New York, married a waitress, got a job as a redcap, and would have settled down forever in a little flat in Harlem, had not some of his friends discovered that he could sing. They persuaded him to join a Red Cap Quartette. Out of that had come this work as a black angel in what turned out to be a Broadway success in the midst of the depression.

Just before the show went on the road, his wife had their first kid, so he needed to hold his job as a singing angel, even if it meant going on tour. But the more he thought about their forthcoming appearance in a Washington theater that wasn't even Jim Crow—but barred Negroes altogether—the madder Logan got. Finally he got so mad that he caused the rest of the cast to organize a strike!

At that distance from Washington, black angels—from tenors to basses, sopranos to blues singers—were up in arms. Everybody in the cast, except God, agreed to strike.

"The idea of a town where colored folks can't even sit in the gallery to see an all-colored show. I ain't gonna work there myself."

"We'll show them white folks we've got spunk for once. We'll pull off the biggest actors' strike you ever seen."

"We sure will."

That was in Philadelphia. In Baltimore their ardor had cooled down a bit and it was all Logan could do to hold his temper as he felt his fellow angels weakening.

"Man, I got a wife to take care of. I can't lose no week's work!"

"I got a wife, too," said Logan, "and a kid besides, but I'm game."

"You ain't a trouper," said another, as he sat in the dressing room putting on his make-up.

"Naw, if you was you'd be used to playing all-white houses. In the old days . . ." said the man who played Methuselah, powdering his gray wig.

"I know all about the old days," said Logan, "when black minstrels blacked up even blacker and made fun of themselves for the benefit of white folks. But who wants to go back to the old days?"

"Anyhow, let's let well enough alone," said Methuselah.

"You guys have got no guts—that's all I can say," said Logan.

"You's just one of them radicals, son, that's what you are," put in the old tenor who played Saul. "We know when we want to strike or don't."

"Listen, then," said Logan to the angels who were putting on their wings by now, as it was near curtain time, "if we can't make it a real strike, then let's make it a general walk-out on the opening night. Strike for one performance anyhow. At least show folks that we won't take it lying down. Show those Washington Negroes we back them up—theoretically, anyhow."

"One day ain't so bad," said a skinny black angel. "I'm with you on a one-day strike."

"Me, too," several others agreed as they crowded into the corridor at curtain time. The actor who played God was standing in the wings in his frock coat.

"Shss-ss!" he said.

Monday in Washington. The opening of that famous white play about black life in a scenic heaven. Original New York cast. Songs as only Negroes can sing them. Uncle Tom come back as God.

Negro Washington wanted to picket the theater, but the police had an injunction against them. Cops were posted for blocks around the playhouse to prevent a riot. Nobody could see God. He was safely housed in the quiet home of a conservative Negro professor, guarded by two detectives. The papers said black radicals had threatened to kidnap him. To kidnap God!

Logan spent the whole day rallying the flagging spirits of his fellow actors, talking to them in their hotel rooms. They were solid for the one-day strike when he was around, and weak when he wasn't. No telling what Washington cops might do to them if they struck. They locked Negroes up for less than that in Washington. Besides, they might get canned, they might lose their pay, they might never get no more jobs on the stage. It was all right to talk about being a man and standing up for your race, and all that—but hell, even an actor has to eat. Besides, God was right. It was a great play, a famous play! They ought to hold up its reputation. It did white folks good to see Negroes in such a play. Logan must be crazy!

"Listen here, you might as well get wise. Ain't nobody gonna strike tonight," one of the men told him about six o'clock in the lobby of the colored Whitelaw Hotel. "You'd just as well give up. You're right. We ain't got no guts."

"I won't give up," said Logan.

When the actors reached the theater, they found it surrounded by cops and the stage was full of detectives. In the lobby there was a long line of people—white, of course—waiting to buy standing room. God arrived with motorcycle cops in front of his car. He had come a little early to address the cast. With him was the white stage manager and a representative of the New York producing office.

They called everybody together on the stage. The Lord wept as he spoke of all his race had borne to get where Negroes are today. Of how they had struggled. Of how they sang. Of how they must keep on struggling and singing—until white folks see the light. A strike would do no good. A strike would only hurt their cause. With sorrow in his heart—but more noble because of it—he would go on with the play. He was sure his actors—his angels—his children—would continue, too.

The white men accompanying God were very solemn, as though hurt to their souls to think what their Negro employees were suffering, but far more hurt to think that Negroes had wanted to jeopardize a week's box-office receipts by a strike! That would really harm everybody!

Behind God and the white managers stood two big detectives.

Needless to say, the Negroes finally went downstairs to put on their wings and make-up. All but Logan. He went downstairs to drag the cast out by force, to make men of darkies, to carry through the strike. But he couldn't. Not alone. Nobody really wanted to strike. Nobody wanted to sacrifice anything for race pride, decency, or elementary human rights. The actors only wanted to keep on appearing in a naïve dialect play about a quaint, funny heaven full of niggers at which white people laughed and wept.

The management sent two detectives downstairs to get Logan. They were taking no chances. Just as the curtain rose they carted him off to jail—for disturbing the peace. The colored angels were all massed in the wings for the opening spiritual when the police took the black boy out, a line of tears running down his cheeks.

Most of the actors *wanted* to think Logan was crying because he was being arrested—but in their souls they knew that was not why he wept.

● *On the Road*

●   *HE WAS* not interested in the snow. When he got off the freight, one early evening during the depression, Sargeant never even noticed the snow. But he must have felt it seeping down his neck, cold, wet, sopping in his shoes. But if you had asked him, he wouldn't have known it was snowing. Sargeant didn't see the snow, not even under the bright lights of the main street, falling white and flaky against the night. He was too hungry, too sleepy, too tired.

The Reverend Mr. Dorset, however, saw the snow when he switched on his porch light, opened the front door of his parsonage, and found standing there before him a big black man with snow on his face, a human piece of night with snow on his face—obviously unemployed.

Said the Reverend Mr. Dorset before Sargeant even realized he'd opened his mouth: "I'm sorry. No! Go right on down this street four blocks and turn to your left, walk up seven and you'll see the Relief Shelter. I'm sorry. No!" He shut the door.

Sargeant wanted to tell the holy man that he had already been to the Relief Shelter, been to hundreds of relief shelters during the depression years, the beds were always gone and supper was over, the place was full, and they drew the color line anyhow. But the minister said, "No," and shut the door. Evidently he didn't want to hear about it. And he *had* a door to shut.

The big black man turned away. And even yet he didn't see the snow, walking right into it. Maybe he sensed it, cold, wet, sticking to his jaws, wet on his black hands, sopping in his shoes. He stopped and stood on the sidewalk hunched over—hungry, sleepy, cold—looking up and down. Then he looked right where he was—in front of a church. Of course! A church! Sure, right next to a parsonage, certainly a church.

It had *two* doors.

Broad white steps in the night all snowy white. Two

high arched doors with slender stone pillars on either
side. And way up, a round lacy window with a stone crucifix in the middle and Christ on the crucifix in stone. All
this was pale in the street lights, solid and stony pale in the
snow.

Sargeant blinked. When he looked up the snow fell into
his eyes. For the first time that night he *saw* the snow. He
shook his head. He shook the snow from his coat sleeves,
felt hungry, felt lost, felt not lost, felt cold. He walked up
the steps of the church. He knocked at the door. No answer.
He tried the handle. Locked. He put his shoulder against
the door and his long black body slanted like a ramrod. He
pushed. With loud rhythmic grunts, like the grunts in a
chain-gang song, he pushed against the door.

"I'm tired . . . Huh! . . . Hongry . . . Uh! . . . I'm
sleepy . . . Huh! I'm cold . . . I got to sleep somewheres,"
Sargeant said. "This here is a church, ain't it? Well, uh!"

He pushed against the door.

Suddenly, with an undue cracking and screaking, the
door began to give way to the tall black Negro who pushed
ferociously against the door.

By now two or three white people had stopped in the
street, and Sargeant was vaguely aware of some of them
yelling at him concerning the door. Three or four more
came running, yelling at him.

"Hey!" they said. "Hey!"

"Un-huh," answered the big tall Negro, "I know it's a
white folks' church, but I got to sleep somewhere." He
gave another lunge at the door. "Huh!"

And the door broke open.

But just when the door gave way, two white cops arrived
in a car, ran up the steps with their clubs and grabbed Sar-

geant. But Sargeant for once had no intention of being pulled or pushed away from the door.

Sargeant grabbed, but not for anything so weak as a broken door. He grabbed for one of the tall stone pillars beside the door, grabbed at it and caught it. And held it. The cops pulled and Sargeant pulled. Most of the people in the street got behind the cops and helped them pull.

"A big black unemployed Negro holding onto our church!" thought the people. "The idea!"

The cops began to beat Sargeant over the head, and nobody protested. But he held on.

And then the church fell down.

Gradually, the big stone front of the church fell down, the walls and the rafters, the crucifix and the Christ. Then the whole thing fell down, covering the cops and the people with bricks and stones and debris. The whole church fell down in the snow.

Sargeant got out from under the church and went walking on up the street with the stone pillar on his shoulder. He was under the impression that he had buried the parsonage and the Reverend Mr. Dorset who said, "No!" So he laughed, and threw the pillar six blocks up the street and went on.

Sargeant thought he was alone, but listening to the crunch, crunch, crunch on the snow of his own footsteps, he heard other footsteps, too, doubling his own. He looked around and there was Christ walking along beside him, the same Christ that had been on the cross on the church—still stone with a rough stone surface, walking along beside him just like he was broken off the cross when the church fell down.

"Well, I'll be dogged," said Sargeant. "This here's the first time I ever seed you off the cross."

"Yes," said Christ, crunching his feet in the snow. "You had to pull the church down to get me off the cross."

"You glad?" said Sargeant.

"I sure am," said Christ.

They both laughed.

"I'm a hell of a fellow, ain't I?" said Sargeant. "Done pulled the church down!"

"You did a good job," said Christ. "They have kept me nailed on a cross for nearly two thousand years."

"Whee-ee-e!" said Sargeant. "I know you are glad to get off."

"I sure am," said Christ.

They walked on in the snow. Sargeant looked at the man of stone.

"And you been up there two thousand years?"

"I sure have," Christ said.

"Well, if I had a little cash," said Sargeant, "I'd show you around a bit."

"I been around," said Christ.

"Yeah, but that was a long time ago."

"All the same," said Christ, "I've been around."

They walked on in the snow until they came to the railroad yards. Sargeant was tired, sweating and tired.

"Where you goin'?" Sargeant said, stopping by the tracks. He looked at Christ. Sargeant said, "I'm just a bum on the road. How about you? Where you goin'?"

"God knows," Christ said, "but I'm leavin' here."

They saw the red and green lights of the railroad yard half veiled by the snow that fell out of the night. Away down the track they saw a fire in a hobo jungle.

"I can go there and sleep," Sargeant said.

"You can?"

"Sure," said Sargeant. "That place ain't got no doors."

Outside the town, along the tracks, there were barren trees and bushes below the embankment, snow-gray in the dark. And down among the trees and bushes there were makeshift houses made out of boxes and tin and old pieces of wood and canvas. You couldn't see them in the dark, but you knew they were there if you'd ever been on the road, if you had ever lived with the homeless and hungry in a depression.

"I'm side-tracking," Sargeant said. "I'm tired."

"I'm gonna make it on to Kansas City," said Christ.

"O.K.," Sargeant said. "So long!"

He went down into the hobo jungle and found himself a place to sleep. He never did see Christ no more. About six A.M. a freight came by. Sargeant scrambled out of the jungle with a dozen or so more hoboes and ran along the track, grabbing at the freight. It was dawn, early dawn, cold and gray.

"Wonder where Christ is by now?" Sargeant thought. "He must-a gone on way on down the road. He didn't sleep in this jungle."

Sargeant grabbed the train and started to pull himself up into a moving coal car, over the edge of a wheeling coal car. But strangely enough, the car was full of cops. The nearest cop rapped Sargeant soundly across the knuckles with his night stick. Wham! Rapped his big black hands for clinging to the top of the car. Wham! But Sargeant did not turn loose. He clung on and tried to pull himself into the car. He hollered at the top of his voice, "Damn it, lemme in this car!"

"Shut up," barked the cop. "You crazy coon!" He rapped Sargeant across the knuckles and punched him in the stomach. "You ain't out in no jungle now. This ain't no train. You in jail."

Wham! across his bare black fingers clinging to the bars of his cell. Wham! between the steel bars low down against his shins.

Suddenly Sargeant realized that he really was in jail. He wasn't on no train. The blood of the night before had dried on his face, his head hurt terribly, and a cop outside in the corridor was hitting him across the knuckles for holding onto the door, yelling and shaking the cell door.

"They must-a took me to jail for breaking down the door last night," Sargeant thought, "that church door."

Sargeant went over and sat on a wooden bench against the cold stone wall. He was emptier than ever. His clothes were wet, clammy cold wet, and shoes sloppy with snow water. It was just about dawn. There he was, locked up behind a cell door, nursing his bruised fingers.

The bruised fingers were his, but not the *door*.

Not the *club*, but the fingers.

"You wait," mumbled Sargeant, black against the jail wall. "I'm gonna break down this door, too."

"Shut up—or I'll paste you one," said the cop.

"I'm gonna break down this door," yelled Sargeant as he stood up in his cell.

Then he must have been talking to himself because he said, "I wonder where Christ's gone? I wonder if he's gone to Kansas City?"

• *Big Meeting*

• *THE* early stars had begun to twinkle in the August night as Bud and I neared the woods. A great many Negroes, old and young, were plodding down the dirt road on foot on their way to the Big Meeting. Long before we came near the lantern-lighted tent we could hear early arrivals singing, clapping their hands lustily and throwing out each word distinct like a drumbeat. Songs like "When the Saints Go Marching Home" and "That Old-time Religion" filled the air.

In the road that ran past the woods, a number of automobiles and buggies belonging to white people had stopped near the tent so that their occupants might listen to the singing. The whites stared curiously through the hickory trees at the rocking figures in the tent. The canvas, except behind the pulpit, was rolled up on account of the heat, and the meeting could easily be seen from the road, so there beneath a tree Bud and I stopped, too. In our teens, we were young and wild and didn't believe much in revivals, so we stayed outside in the road where we could smoke and laugh like the white folks. But both Bud's mother and mine were under the tent singing, actively a part of the services. Had they known we were near, they would certainly have come out and dragged us in.

From frequent attendance since childhood at these Big Meetings held each summer in the South, we knew the services were divided into three parts. The testimonials and the song-service came first. This began as soon as two or three people were gathered together, continuing until the minister himself arrived. Then the sermon followed, with its accompanying songs and shouts from the audience. Then the climax came with the calling of the lost souls to the mourners' bench, and the prayers for sinners and backsliders. This was where Bud and I would leave. We were having too good a time being sinners, and we didn't want to be saved—not yet, anyway.

When we arrived, old Aunt Ibey Davis was just starting a familiar song:

> *Where shall I be when that first trumpet sound?*
> *Lawdy, where shall I be when it sound so loud?*

The rapidly increasing number of worshipers took up the tune in full volume sending a great flood of melody billowing beneath the canvas roof. With heads back, feet and hands patting time, they repeated the chorus again and again. And each party of new arrivals swung into rhythm as they walked up the aisle by the light of the dim oil lanterns hanging from the tent poles.

Standing there at the edge of the road beneath a big tree, Bud and I watched the people as they came—keeping our eyes open for the girls. Scores of Negroes from the town and nearby villages and farms came drawn by the music and the preaching. Some were old and gray-headed; some in the prime of life; some mere boys and girls; and many little barefooted children. It was the twelfth night of the Big Meeting. They came from miles around to bathe their souls in a sea of song, to shout and cry and moan before the flow of Reverend Braswell's eloquence, and to pray for all the sinners in the county who had not yet seen the light. Although it was a colored folks' meeting, whites liked to come and sit outside in the road in their cars and listen. Sometimes there would be as many as ten or twelve parties of whites parked there in the dark, smoking and listening, and enjoying themselves, like Bud and I, in a not very serious way.

Even while old Aunt Ibey Davis was singing, a big red buick drove up and parked right behind Bud and me beneath the tree. It was full of white people, and we recognized the driver as Mr. Parkes, the man who owned the drugstore in town where colored people couldn't buy a glass of soda at the fountain.

> *It will sound so loud it will wake up the dead!*
> *Lawdy, where shall I be when it sound?*

"You'll hear some good singing out here," Mr. Parkes said to a woman in the car with him.

"I always did love to hear darkies singing," she answered from the back seat.

Bud nudged me in the ribs at the word *darkie*.

"I hear 'em," I said, sitting down on one of the gnarled roots of the tree and pulling out a cigarette.

The song ended as an old black woman inside the tent got up to speak. "I rise to testify dis evenin' fo' Jesus!" she said. "Ma Saviour an' ma Redeemer an' de chamber wherein I resusticates ma soul. Pray fo' me, brothers and sisters. Let yo' mercies bless me in all I do an' yo' prayers go with me on each travelin' voyage through dis land."

"Amen! Hallelujah!" cried my mother.

Just in front of us, near the side of the tent, a woman's clear soprano voice began to sing:

> *I am a po' pilgrim of sorrow*
> *Out in this wide world alone . . .*

Soon others joined with her and the whole tent was singing:

> *Sometimes I am tossed and driven,*
> *Sometimes I don't know where to go . . .*

"Real pretty, ain't it?" said the white woman in the car behind us.

> *But I've heard of a city called heaven*
> *And I've started to make it my home.*

When the woman finished her song she rose and told how her husband left her with six children, her mother died in a poorhouse, and the world had always been against her—but still she was going on!

"My, she's had a hard time," giggled the woman in the car.

"Sure has," laughed Mr. Parkes, "to hear her tell it."

And the way they talked made gooseflesh come out on my skin.

"Trials and tribulations surround me—but I'm goin' on," the woman in the tent cried. Shouts and exclamations of approval broke out all over the congregation.

"Praise God!"

"Bless His Holy Name!"

"That's right, sister!"

"Devils beset me—but I'm goin' on!" said the woman. "I ain't got no friends—but I'm goin' on!"

"Jesus yo' friend, sister! Jesus yo' friend!" came the answer.

"God bless Jesus! I'm goin' on!"

"Dat's right!" cried Sister Mabry, Bud's mother, bouncing in her seat and flinging her arms outward. "Take all this world, but gimme Jesus!"

"Look at mama," Bud said half amused, sitting there beside me smoking. "She's getting happy."

"Whoo-ooo-o-o! Great Gawd-a-Mighty!" yelled old man Walls near the pulpit. "I can't hold it dis evenin'! Dis mawnin', dis evenin', dis mawnin', Lawd!"

"Pray for me—cause I'm goin' on!" said the woman. In the midst of the demonstration she had created she sat down exhausted, her armpits wet with sweat and her face covered with tears.

"Did you hear her, Jehover?" someone asked.

"Yes! He heard her! Halleloo!" came the answer.
"Dis mawnin', dis evenin', dis mawnin', Lawd!"
Brother Nace Eubanks began to line a song:

> *Must Jesus bear his cross alone*
> *An' all de world go free?*

Slowly they sang it line by line. Then the old man rose and told of a vision that had come to him long ago on that day when he had been changed from a sinner to a just man.

"I was layin' in ma bed," he said, "at de midnight hour twenty-two years past at 714 Pine Street in dis here city when a snow-white sheep come in ma room an' stood behind de wash bowl. Dis here sheep, hit spoke to me wid tongues o' fiah an' hit said, 'Nace, git up! Git up, an' come wid me!' Yes, suh! He had a light round 'bout his head like a moon, an' wings like a dove, an' he walked on hoofs o' gold an' dis sheep hit said, 'I once were lost, but now I'm saved, an' you kin be like me!' Yes, suh! An' ever since dat night, brothers an' sisters, I's been a chile o' de Lamb! Pray fo' me!"

"Help him, Jesus!" Sister Mabry shouted.

"Amen!" chanted Deacon Laws. "Amen! Amen!"

> *Glory! Hallelujah!*
> *Let de halleluian roll!*
> *I'll sing ma Saviour's praises far an' wide!*

It was my mother's favorite song, and she sang it like a paean of triumph, rising from her seat.

"Look at ma," I said to Bud, knowing that she was about to start her nightly shouting.

"Yah," Bud said. "I hope she don't see me while she's standing up there, or she'll come out here and make us go up to the mourners' bench."

"We'll leave before that," I said.

> *I've opened up to heaven*
> *All de windows of ma soul,*
> *An' I'm livin' on de halleluian side!*

Rocking proudly to and fro as the second chorus boomed and swelled beneath the canvas, mama began to clap her hands, her lips silent now in this sea of song she had started, her head thrown back in joy—for my mother was a great shouter. Stepping gracefully to the beat of the music, she moved out toward the center aisle into a cleared space. Then she began to spring on her toes with little short rhythmical hops. All the way up the long aisle to the pulpit gently she leaped to the clap-clap of hands, the pat of feet, and the steady booming song of her fellow worshipers. Then mama began to revolve in a dignified circle, slowly, as a great happiness swept her gleaming black features, and her lips curved into a smile.

> *I've opened up to heaven*
> *All de windows of my soul . . .*

Mama was dancing before the Lord with her eyes closed, her mouth smiling, and her head held high.

> *I'm livin' on de halleluian side!*

As she danced she threw her hands upward away from her breasts as though casting off all the cares of the world.

Just then the white woman in Mr. Parkes' car behind us laughed, "My Lord, John, it's better than a show!"

Something about the way she laughed made my blood boil. That was *my mother* dancing and shouting. Maybe it was better than a show, but nobody had any business laughing at her, least of all white people.

I looked at Bud, but he didn't say anything. Maybe he was thinking how often we, too, made fun of the shouters, laughing at our parents as though they were crazy—but deep down inside us we understood why they came to Big Meeting. Working all day all their lives for white folks, they *had* to believe there was a "Halleluian Side."

I looked at mama standing there singing, and I thought about how many years she had prayed and shouted and praised the Lord at church meetings and revivals, then came home for a few hours' sleep before getting up at dawn to go cook and scrub and clean for others. And I didn't want any white folks, especially whites who wouldn't let a Negro drink a glass of soda in their drug-store or give one a job, sitting in a car laughing at mama.

"Gimme a cigarette, Bud. If these dopes behind us say any more, I'm gonna get up and tell 'em something they won't like."

"To hell with 'em," Bud answered.

I leaned back against the gnarled roots of the tree by the road and inhaled deeply. The white people were silent again in their car, listening to the singing. In the dark I couldn't see their faces to tell if they were still amused or not. But that was mostly what they wanted out of Negroes —work and fun—without paying for it, I thought, work and fun.

To a great hand-clapping, body-rocking, foot-patting rhythm, mama was repeating the chorus over and over. Sisters leaped and shouted and perspiring brothers walked the aisles bowing left and right, beating time, shaking hands, laughing aloud for joy, and singing steadily when, at the back of the tent, the Reverend Duke Braswell arrived.

A tall, powerful, jet-black man, he moved with long steps through the center of the tent, his iron-gray hair uncovered, his green-black coat jim-swinging to his knees, his fierce eyes looking straight toward the altar. Under his arm he carried a Bible.

Once on the platform, he stood silently wiping his brow with a large white handkerchief while the singing swirled around him. Then he sang, too, his voice roaring like a cyclone, his white teeth shining. Finally he held up his palms for silence and the song gradually lowered to a hum, hum, hum, hands and feet patting, bodies still moving. At last, above the broken cries of the shouters and the undertones of song, the minister was able to make himself heard.

"Brother Garner, offer up a prayer."

Reverend Braswell sank on his knees and every back bowed. Brother Garner, with his head in his hands, lifted his voice against a background of moans:

"Oh, Lawd, we comes befo' you dis evenin' wid fear an' tremblin'—unworthy as we is to enter yo' house an' speak yo' name. We comes befo' you, Lawd, cause we knows you is mighty an' powerful in all de lands, an' great above de stars, an' bright above de moon. Oh, Lawd, you is bigger den de world. You holds de sun in yo' right hand an' de mornin' star in yo' left, an' we po' sinners ain't nothin', not even so much as a grain o' sand beneath yo' feet. Yet we calls on you dis evenin' to hear us, Lawd, to send down yo' sweet Son Jesus to walk wid us in our sorrows to comfort us on our weary road cause sometimes we don't know which-a-way to turn! We pray you dis evenin', Lawd, to look down at our wanderin' chilluns what's gone from home. Look down in St. Louis, Lawd, an' look in Memphis, an' look down in Chicago if they's usin' Thy name in vain dis evenin', if they's gamblin' tonight, Lawd, if they's doin' any ways wrong—reach down an' pull 'em up, Lawd, an' say, 'Come wid me, cause I am de Vine an' de Husbandman an' de gate dat leads to Glory!' "

Remembering sons in faraway cities, "Help him, Jesus!" mothers cried.

"Whilst you's lookin' down on us dis evenin', keep a mighty eye on de sick an' de 'flicked. Ease Sister Hightower, Lawd, layin' in her bed at de pint o' death. An' bless Bro' Carpenter what's come out to meetin' here dis evenin' in spite o' his broken arm from fallin' off de roof. An' Lawd, aid de pastor dis evenin' to fill dis tent wid yo' Spirit, an' to make de sinners tremble an' backsliders shout, an' dem dat is widout de church to come to de moaners' bench an' find rest in Jesus! We ask Thee all dese favors dis evenin'. Also to guide us an' bless us wid Thy bread an' give us Thy wine to drink fo' Christ de Holy Saviour's sake, our Shelter an' our Rock. Amen!"

There's not a friend like de lowly Jesus . . .

Some sister began, high and clear after the passion of the prayer,

No, not one! . . . No, not one!

Then the preacher took his text from the open Bible. "Ye now therefore have sorrow: but I will see you again, and your hearts shall rejoice, and your joy no man taketh from you."

He slammed shut the Holy Book and walked to the edge of the platform. "That's what Jesus said befo' he went to the cross, children—'I will see you again, and yo' hearts shall rejoice!' "

"Yes, sir!" said the brothers and sisters. " 'Deed he did!"

Then the minister began to tell the familiar story of the death of Christ. Standing in the dim light of the smoking oil lanterns, he sketched the life of the man who had had power over multitudes.

"Power," the minister said. "Power! Without money and without titles, without position, he had power! And that power went out to the poor and afflicted. For Jesus said, 'The first shall be last, and the last shall be first.' "

"He sho did!" cried Bud's mother.

"Hallelujah!" mama agreed loudly. "Glory be to God!"

"Then the big people of the land heard about Jesus," the preacher went on, "the chief priests and the scribes, the politicians, the bootleggers, and the bankers—and they begun to conspire against Jesus because *He had power*! This Jesus with His twelve disciples preachin' in Galilee. Then came that eve of the Passover, when he set down with His friends to eat and drink of the vine and the settin' sun fell behind the hills of Jerusalem. And Jesus knew that ere the cock crew Judas would betray Him, and Peter would say, 'I know Him not,' and all alone by Hisself He would go to His death. Yes, sir, He knew! So He got up from the table and went into the garden to pray. In this hour of trouble, Jesus went to pray!"

Away at the back of the tent some old sister began to sing:

> *Oh, watch with me one hour*
> *While I go yonder and pray . . .*

And the crowd took up the song, swelled it, made its melody fill the hot tent while the minister stopped talking to wipe his face with his white handkerchief.

Then to the humming undertone of the song, he continued, "They called it Gethsemane—that garden where Jesus fell down on His face in the grass and cried to the Father, 'Let this bitter hour pass from me! Oh, God, let this hour pass.' Because He was still a young man who did not want to die, He rose up and went back into the house —but His friends was all asleep. While Jesus prayed, His friends done gone to sleep! But, 'Sleep on,' he said, 'for the hour is at hand.' Jesus said, 'Sleep on.'"

"Sleep on, sleep on," chanted the crowd, repeating the words of the minister.

"He was not angry with them. But as Jesus looked out of the house, He saw that garden alive with men carryin' lanterns and swords and staves, and the mob was everywhere. So He went to the door. Then Judas come out from among the crowd, the traitor Judas, and kissed Him on the cheek—Oh, bitter friendship! And the soldiers with handcuffs fell upon the Lord and took Him prisoner.

"The disciples was awake by now, Oh, yes! But they fled away because they was afraid. And the mob carried Jesus off.

"Peter followed Him from afar, followed Jesus in chains till they come to the palace of the high priest. There Peter went in, timid and afraid, to see the trial. He set in the back of the hall. Peter listened to the lies they told about Christ—and didn't dispute 'em. He watched the high priest spit in Christ's face—and made no move. He saw 'em smite Him with the palms of they hands—and Peter uttered not a word for his poor mistreated Jesus."

"Not a word! . . . Not a word! . . . Not a word!"

"And when the servants of the high priest asked Peter, 'Does you know this man?' he said, 'I do not!'"

"And when they asked him a second time, he said, 'No!'"

"And yet a third time, 'Do you know Jesus?'"

"And Peter answered with an oath, 'I told you, No!'"

"Then the cock crew."

"De cock crew!" cried Aunt Ibey Davis. "De cock crew! Oh, ma Lawd! De cock crew!"

"The next day the chief priests taken counsel against Jesus to put Him to death. They brought Him before Pilate, and Pilate said, 'What evil hath he done?'"

"But the people cried, 'Crucify Him!' because they didn't care. So Pilate called for water and washed his hands.

"The soldiers made sport of Jesus where He stood in the Council Hall. They stripped Him naked, and put a crown of thorns on His head, a red robe about His body, and a reed from the river in His hands.

"They said, 'Ha! Ha! So you're the King! Ha! Ha!' And they bowed down in mockery before Him, makin' fun of Jesus.

"Some of the guards threw wine in His face. Some of the guards was drunk and called Him out o' His name—and nobody said, 'Stop! That's Jesus!'"

The Reverend Duke Braswell's face darkened with horror as he pictured the death of Christ. "Oh, yes! Peter denied Him because he was afraid. Judas betrayed Him for thirty pieces of silver. Pilate said, 'I wash my hands—take Him and kill Him.'

"And His friends fled away! . . . Have mercy on Jesus! . . . His friends done fled away!"

"His friends!"

"His friends done fled away!"

The preacher chanted, half moaning his sentences, not speaking them. His breath came in quick, short gasps with an indrawn, "Umn!" between each rapid phrase. Perspiration poured down his face as he strode across the platform wrapped in this drama that he saw in the very air before his eyes. Peering over the heads of his audience out into the darkness, he began the ascent to Golgotha, describing the taunting crowd at Christ's heels and the heavy cross on His shoulders.

"Then a black man named Simon, blacker than me, come and took the cross and bore it for Him. Umn!

"Then Jesus were standin' alone on a high hill, in the broilin' sun, while they put the crosses in the ground. No water to cool His throat! No tree to shade His achin' head! Nobody to say a friendly word to Jesus! Umn!

"Alone, in that crowd on the hill of Golgotha, with two thieves bound and dyin', and the murmur of the mob all around. Umn!

"But Jesus never said a word! Umn!

"They laid they hands on Him, and they tore the clothes from His body—and then, and then," loud as a thunderclap, the minister's voice broke through the little tent, "they raised Him to the cross!"

A great wail went up from the crowd. Bud and I sat entranced in spite of ourselves, forgetting to smoke. Aunt Ibey Davis wept. Sister Mabry moaned. In their car behind us the white people were silent as the minister went on:

> They brought four long iron nails
> And put one in the palm of His left hand.
> The hammer said . . . Bam!
> They put one in the palm of His right hand.
> The hammer said . . . Bam!
> They put one through His left foot . . . Bam!
> And one through His right foot . . . Bam!

"Don't drive it!" a woman screamed. "Don't drive them nails! For Christ's sake! Oh! Don't drive 'em!"

And they left my Jesus on the cross!
Nails in His hands! Nails in His feet!
Sword in His side! Thorns circlin' His head!
Mob cussin' and hootin' my Jesus! Umn!
The spit of the mob in His face! Umn!
His body hangin' on the cross! Umn!
Gimme piece of His garment for a souvenir! Umn!
Castin' lots for His garments! Umn!
Blood from His wounded side! Umn!
Streamin' down His naked legs! Umn!
Droppin' in the dust—umn—
That's what they did to my Jesus!
They stoned Him first, they stoned Him!
Called Him everything but a child of God.
Then they lynched Him on the cross.

In song I heard my mother's voice cry:

Were you there when they crucified my Lord?
Were you there when they nailed Him to the tree?

The Reverend Duke Braswell stretched wide his arms against the white canvas of the tent. In the yellow light his body made a cross-like shadow on the canvas.

Oh, it makes me to tremble, tremble!
Were you there when they crucified my Lord?

"Let's go," said the white woman in the car behind us. "This is too much for me!" They started the motor and drove noisily away in a swirl of dust.

"Don't go," I cried from where I was sitting at the root of the tree. "Don't go," I shouted, jumping up. "They're about to call for sinners to come to the mourners' bench. Don't go!" But their car was already out of earshot.

I didn't realize I was crying until I tasted my tears in my mouth.